KATHARINE

JAY

BACON

MARGARET K. MCELDERRY BOOKS

ALSO BY KATHARINE JAY BACON
Pip and Emma
Shadow and Light
(MARGARET K. MCELDERRY BOOKS)

— ♣ —

Margaret K. McElderry Books
An imprint of Simon & Schuster Children's Publishing Division
1230 Avenue of the Americas
New York, NY 10020

Book design by Michael Nelson
The text of this book was set in New Caledonia.
Printed in the United States of America
First Edition
10 9 8 7 6 5 4 3 2 1
Library of Congress Cataloging-in-Publication Data
Bacon, Katharine Jay.
Finn / Katharine Jay Bacon.—1st ed.
p. cm.
Summary: Unable to speak after his parents and sister are killed in a plane crash,
fifteen-year-old Finn comes to stay with his grandmother on her Vermont farm,
where his friendship with a neighbor, the activities of
local drug dealers, and the actions of a hybrid wolf force him to
deal with his grief.
ISBN 0-689-82216-2
[1. Grief—Fiction. 2. Mutism, Elective—Fiction. 3. Cocaine—Fiction.] I. Title.
PZ7.B1344Fi 1998
[Fic]—dc21 98-10778

For my grandchildren:

Sam
Eliza
Sybil
Justin
Dan
Ben
Rebecca
Jack
Sam
Arthur
Luke
Bob
Kate
Peter
Binny
Frances
John
Joe
Phil
Lucy
Grace
Harry
Charlie
George
Noah
and Sofia

with love from GaGa

Chapter 1

FINN'S EYES FLEW OPEN. He sat up and with his good hand groped for something in the darkness. *Someone called my name,* he thought, and he tried to answer, but no sound came. *Am I in or out of this nightmare?* His heart beat so loud and so fast he thought surely that was why he could not see. If only his heart would slow down he would be able to figure out where he was.

The room smelled familiar. Then, as the pale square of a window emerged out of the black, he began to remember. His eyes felt their way around the room: bureau over there, door straight ahead, oh, yes, of course, a chair to the right. So he was in the attic room at Riverview Farm. Now that he knew for sure, he slumped back against the headboard, waiting for the last of his dream to evaporate, wishing he could banish the sound of the voice calling, *"Finn!"*

Almost imperceptibly the room lightened around him. The panes of the window went from pearl gray to—suddenly—pale pink. A shaft of sunlight entered and seemed to move deliberately from one object to the next, until the whole room was suffused in the first light of day.

Slowly, Finn rose from the bed and limped across to the window, surprised to find that this year he had to duck his head under the eaves. Laying his forehead against the cool pane, his throat still aching from wanting to answer that call, he stared down at the farm. How familiar it was: barn, fences, enormous maples rustling now in the light dawn breeze. How he loved it, and how he wished he wasn't here. He shrugged and turned back toward the bed and lay down again.

The rising sun cleared the hills across the river and slowly brought the longest day of the year to life. Down in the barnyard of Riverview Farm an old gray mare named Belle stirred and opened her long-lashed eyes, three other horses started to move toward the pasture, goats bleated sleepily, and five fat hens waddled out into the sun.

The mare stood unmoving for a few minutes, watching as the other horses began to graze: old Hiram and Horace, the retired draft horses, and Daisy, Belle's last filly. Daisy was two. Bay and beautiful, she demanded and got a great deal of attention from the other horses.

Suddenly the old mare stiffened. Her ears shot to

attention, pointing toward the far end of the pasture. There something or someone moved. Belle took two steps forward and her nostrils flared with suspicion as a stranger strode across the field, climbed the fence and walked along the edge of the thick pinewood on the other side. There he stopped, bent low, and brushed aside the lower branches of a pine. Belle whickered to the other horses to look, but just as they raised their heads, the intruder climbed back over the fence, walked hurriedly across the pasture, scaled the far fence, and heaved himself into a pickup at the side of the dirt road. He slammed the door and drove off in a swirl of dust.

Two minutes later a cat named Monica slipped into the barn. She stood for a moment in the sunny doorway, listening for mice. Hearing none, she climbed one of the old cow stanchions and from there leaped nimbly up to a beam near the shed door. She was a calico cat, but all the white was on her stomach so she was nearly invisible lying inside the big dark barn. Slowly, luxuriously, she began to lick each paw, lingering over her morning bath as though she were simply waiting for something to happen.

Finn sat at the kitchen table, watching his grandmother slice bread and allowing her stream of words to flow over and around him. The room and everything in it were so familiar that he felt as though he were watching an old movie: Gram in jeans and checked shirt, gray hair pulled into a bun on the top of her head, hands constantly moving. Teenager slouched at the kitchen table, waiting for breakfast. Sun pouring in the big eastern window. Mick's old dog blanket still under the coal stove. Kettle beginning to whistle . . .

Trouble was, that kid at the table didn't belong in this movie. It was as though he'd stepped in as an understudy for the real boy. This one *looked* like Gram's fifteen-year-old grandson, but he had a scar that ran from his forehead to his cheek, just missing the eye; the scar left a narrow path through the eyebrow. This kid had a cast on his left ankle and wore a black glove on his right hand. And this one's angular face, with its high cheekbones and black-lashed eyes, had a fierce, hunted look that the old Finn never wore.

Finn sighed. No, this was no movie. He was Finn, and Gram was Gram, and yesterday evening they'd arrived at Riverview Farm. Just the two of them. The way his grandmother kept talking was like someone offering a drowning swimmer a lifeline. Finn knew she did not expect an answer, only that she hoped and prayed—last night he actually heard her asking God— that someday, out of the blue, he would speak again.

The telephone rang and he jumped.

"Hello," said his grandmother. "Oh, Mylin, my dear. I was going to call you . . . We only got back late yesterday . . . We had to wait for Finn's new cast to be fitted, and there was so much to do . . . after the service . . ." Her voice wavered but went on, "Yes, out there— in Finn's father's family plot . . . Finn doesn't . . . Oh, you heard . . .Yes, he'll stay with me . . . Yes, I know . . . a miracle . . ."

Finn watched her as she talked to their neighbor. Come to think of it, she didn't look like the old Gram, either. Her face was as drawn as when she appeared in the door of his hospital room three endless weeks ago. He stopped listening and moved slowly to the old rocker near the window. The sun was well up now, the shadows of the aged maples much shorter than they were at dawn. The barnyard at the foot of the slope looked so peaceful on this fresh June morning that Finn stared at it as though he had never seen it before. It made no sense. How could this little piece of the world look so gentle and light when Finn's real world was so violent and black? He heard his grandmother hang up the telephone and speak his name.

"That was Mylin Hatch—you remember her? In the brown house up the road?"

Finn knew she didn't expect an answer.

"Their daughter's Julia, Penny's friend . . . remember?"

Julia . . . Penny . . . If only she wouldn't say their names, he might be able to squash the past out of sight. He locked his jaw and kept staring out the window until he felt his grandmother's hand like a claw on his arm. She clutched him hard and he turned to face her.

"*Remember?*" she asked, half-fierce, half-pleading.

What is the matter with you? he thought furiously. *Do you think I've lost my memory, too?* He avoided her eye and nodded.

"Julia's been coming over here a lot lately when she's not baby-sitting. She's begun working seriously with that two-year-old filly of Belle's. The thing is,

Finn, she likes helping me out and she wants to keep on coming over. This being Saturday, she'd like to work with Daisy this morning and do chores this afternoon, but her mother doesn't know if it's okay with you . . ."

Finn pulled himself to his feet, reached for his crutch, and started for the door. *"What do I care?"* he wanted to say, but he couldn't. For the life of him he couldn't, and that damn pain in his throat was getting worse. He had to get out of here.

At the foot of the stairs he heard his grandmother call, "I told Mylin it was fine by us."

Back in his room under the eaves, the room he'd slept in for four weeks every summer of his life, this Finn-not-Finn threw himself on his bed. The moment he lay flat the nightmare began to gather again.

Walk through it, he told himself. That's what the doctor told him in Cody.

"You won't be out of hell until you walk all the way through it," he'd said.

And so, as sweat turned the palm of his good hand cold and prickled the gloved one, and as his heart doubled its beat, Finn closed his eyes and tried once again to walk through it.

The small airport was nestled right at the foot of the Absaroka Range, south and west of Cody, Wyoming. Only private planes used the airport—single-engined Cessnas and Pipers, mostly. Occasionally you'd see a twin-engined Baron taking off, but rarely, because the runway was short and the mountains loomed so close.

Finn's mother and father and sister were already in the four-seater when he ambled across the tarmac, licking the root beer Popsicle he'd insisted on buying in the little shedlike office. He hadn't found a root beer Popsicle since last year. They must have gone out of style in Wyoming. Finn's father didn't want to lose time—the woman in the office had confirmed the weather report of a front moving rapidly eastward—and he had started to protest when he saw Finn searching in the locker. But Finn just stuck his head farther in and kept looking until he found what he wanted. It seemed as good a way as any to test his father's patience.

When he finally came out of the office, the noise of the plane's idling engine sounded puny in the vast Wyoming landscape. The sky had turned gray. Wind tugged at the scarf of the woman who stood in the office door, waving good-bye. He couldn't decide whether to throw his Popsicle stick on the ground, even though the woman was watching, or bring it into the plane, knowing his father hated trash . . .

"Hurry up, Finn," yelled Penny, so of course he stopped to scrub industriously at a glob of melted popsicle on his shirtfront for as long as he dared.

"Come on, son," his father's even voice carried over the noise of the engine. "The Flight Service Station says we may hit weather in the mountains. We have no time to lose."

Finn finished the last lick of Popsicle, jammed the stick into his pocket, and jogged to the plane. He knew *when not to push too far; this was no time to fool around with his father. It had taken a little while over the past couple of years to work it out between them, but he knew what voice meant what. Flight Service reports meant business. His mother and sister were in the back seats, so he strapped himself in next to his father, hoping his mother was sitting back there by choice and not because he'd kept them waiting. He could feel Penny glaring at the back of his neck and started working on a witty put-down to whatever she said next.*

On his bed in the attic Finn opened his eyes. The sun had warmed the little room. The roots of his thick dark hair were wet with sweat, but his face felt like ice and his mouth was dry and he couldn't even count his heart rate.

What did *Penny say next?* When he couldn't remember, a wave of familiar anxiety began to gather momentum. It started in the pit of his stomach and spread out from there the way air fills a balloon, until Finn thought he'd burst. The doctor in Cody told him how important it was to bring it all up if he ever wanted to talk again. Oh, God, but was it worth it? Was it worth laying it all out, like vomit?

He rolled out of bed onto his good foot and hopped painfully to the bureau. Anything was better than just lying there trying to remember and forget at the same time. At the sight of his face in the mirror, Finn froze. Who was this person staring at him, hair damp and tangled, slashed brow stitched together? Whose wild eyes were those?

"To find your way back, walk through it, step-by-step. Every detail," that doctor had counseled. "*Lean into it.*"

Finn leaned against the bureau and stared at the face in the mirror, appalled, his mind a blank.

What did Penny say next? I can't remember. He wanted to groan, but the groan stuck fast—and silent—in his throat.

Julia Hatch swung off her bicycle and propped it against the side of the house. Before going in the kitchen door, she stopped to gaze fondly at Daisy grazing in the pasture. Then, reluctantly, she turned her gaze away from the pasture and prepared herself to face Finn and his grandmother for the first time since the accident. Letting the screen door close quietly behind her, she stood for a moment in the kitchen doorway watching the woman who might just as well have been her grandmother, too. Ever since she'd known Finn and Penny—which was as long as she could remember—Julia had called her Gram. She was at the sink, with her back to the door, and Julia could see a difference in the way she stood, head down, shoulders low.

"Hi, Gram," she said.

"Julia. There you are." Gram turned. "I didn't hear you come in." The voice so tired it was almost a whisper.

Gram laid down her dish towel and started to open her arms, but just then they both heard Finn limping across the hall. Instinctively they froze and turned to face the door as he lurched into the kitchen.

Finn took one look at Julia and started to spin around on his crutch, but Julia said evenly, as though they'd seen each other the day before, "Hi, Finn, I've come to lunge Daisy. Do you want to come down to the barn with me?"

Wildly he shook his head and retreated back into the hall.

When they heard him stumbling up the stairs, Julia and Gram looked at each other.

"Oh, Gram, it's awful."

"He can't talk. Not a word since it happened," said Gram, wiping her eyes.

"Why?"

"The doctor out there said it was shock. He said Finn was traumatized."

"I knew it would be hard, seeing him," said Julia bleakly. "I didn't think it would be this bad. He looks awful. I could hardly believe my eyes. He doesn't even look like Finn."

Gram put some cups in the cupboard. *She looks old,* thought Julia. *And tired. And very, very sad.*

Then she said, "You know what, Gram? I'm going home now—maybe you'll get some rest. I think I'll skip Daisy this morning. I'll be back to help load those hay bales after lunch."

It can get hot in Vermont at noon, even in June—especially after a hard winter and a short spring. As the sun reached its peak in the sky, the tractor pulling the hay baler in the meadow ceased, as though done in by the heat. Even the birds took refuge, leaving only insects to hum away in the glare of the day. The four horses gathered in the shade of the long shed that ran along the south side of the barn. The western end was fenced off for the three goats who had their own smaller pasture between the house and the barn. Around the corner of the eastern end was the hen yard, empty now, for with the rising heat the five fat hens waddled back to the old calving pen where they slept at night.

A young man entered this cool lower level of the barn, sat down on a sawhorse, and opened his lunch pail. His forearms were greasy with sweat, dirty blond hair clung wetly to his head, and his face was red from the heat of the sun. He was hardly more than a boy. Hay chaff covered his neck and arms and coated his jeans. After gulping at the thermos in his lunch box, he set it down with a sigh and then jumped with surprise as another man blocked the sunlight at the door.

"Well, well, well, there's my little buddy Jack," he said.

"Wha—who—? Oh, Pinky, it's you. Jeez, man, you scared me. What you doin' here, anyways? Rafe said—"

"I needed to talk to you. Saw the tractor out there, figured you'd come in outta the heat. You about done hayin' here?"

Pinky was a shapeless man in his early thirties. He had an indefinite face, small eyes, and thin reddish hair. He sniffed and wiped his nose on the back of his freckled hand.

"Yeah," said Jack. "I'm done now. The old lady said she could handle the last load of bales. But"—Jack looked sharply at the man in the doorway—"you better get in here, out of sight. Rafe'll kill you if he thinks anyone saw me talking to you. Kill the both of us."

"Ah, screw Rafe. I come to tell you I found a new way up to the drop. C'mere."

He dragged Jack to his feet and led him to the shed door.

"See that pinewood?" he said, pointing to the far end of the pasture.

Jack nodded.

"Well, just to the right of the gate, 'bout twenty or thirty yards, there's an old path. I bet you anythin' it leads to the well."

"So what, Pinky? Rafe told me to meet him tonight on some trail up the other side of that hill. Said he'd show me the drop then."

Pinky rubbed at his runny nose. His hand shook slightly. From up at the house came the sound of a screen door slamming. A woman's voice called, "Here, puss, come Monica, puss, puss," and from her high beam above the two men, the calico cat dropped silently at their feet and skittered through the door.

Jack jumped. "Listen, Pinky, forget about that trail and get the hell *out* of here—" His teenage voice broke with anxiety.

"Aw, take it easy. That old woman ain't gonna come down to the barn in this heat, anyways, and so what if she does? She don't know me from Adam, and you only work here come haying."

"Yeah, but that grandson of hers's goin' to the high school with me next fall—"

"What grandson? I thought she lived all alone—"

"You mean you didn't hear? Jeez, Pinky, the whole town's talkin' about it—"

"Hear what?"

"About the plane crash. Whole family wiped out, except him."

The horses' long pasture sloped upward from the river valley and ended at the edge of a dense pinewood. It was a clearly defined three-acre square, with patches of open land on all four sides. Over thirty years ago the state's Department of Agriculture had sent Finn's grandparents a crate of tiny pine seedlings to plant as part of an experiment in erosion control for hilltop pastures. They were meant to have been thinned out, but work on the farm kept the couple too busy to do so. Fifteen years later Finn's grandfather died. Time passed, and now the trees grew so close together that sunlight penetrated them only at noon. Even at noon it never reached the ground, but only lit the upper boughs and dappled the top halves of the long dark trunks.

A thick carpet of pine needles covered the floor of the wood, so thick that if a human had been able to walk among the pines, he or she would not have made a sound. But no grown person could walk upright through the pinewood. Even a child would have difficulty, because the bare dead lower branches were tangled one with another like a web. Years ago Finn and Penny and Julia had tried having a club there. They had spent a week making a path—snapping and sawing off dead twigs and branches until they reached the site of an abandoned springhouse.

Only traces of the wooden frame remained. The well itself looked very much the same as when it had supplied water to the farm: a circle of fieldstones about four feet in diameter and about four feet high, but it had long since run dry, showing the bottom covered with stones and pine needles. There the children had built themselves a fort, using a rope ladder to climb in and out. They made up games having to do with Indian raids; but as the web of branches was so dense, they soon found the Indians had no way to travel except by the path. The whole scheme lost its glamour and they abandoned the fort.

It was always quiet in the dark wood; birds did not settle there, and moose were just too big. But it was the perfect refuge for other wildlife. Each hunting season families of deer gathered to hide. Last year a small black bear had wintered in the pinewood. Coyotes came and went; in May a family of four settled in the eastern end—father, mother, and two year-old pups. Skunks, raccoons, and other small creatures all sought refuge from time to time among the densely planted trees. Only one lived there permanently, in a den hidden deep in the western slope of the wood.

He was a hybrid: half dog, half wolf. His tail was as bushy as a fox's and his coat a thick rich mixture of tawny grays and browns. Broad of brow and chest, with powerful hindquarters and a distinctive wolflike gait, he was almost twice as big as a coyote—though often taken for one—and half again as heavy as a German shepherd.

Four years ago a family vacationing in Montana met a breeder who had raised a litter of hybrid pups. Elated at the idea of owning a wolf, they had brought one back to their home in Vermont in a cage and named him Toq. But it soon was clear to them and to him that his wolf self could not lead a domestic life. After three months he scaled the fence meant to imprison him and found his way over hundreds of miles to the unculled pinewood at Riverview Farm, where he settled. For nearly four years he had foraged for himself through all the seasons, surviving one of the bitterest winters in memory, killing only what he needed to survive, and remaining invisible to all but the sharpest human eye. Now in the heat of the long summer afternoon, he lay panting quietly in his den in the pinewood, always and forever alone.

In the late afternoon Finn came into the cool lower floor of the barn. He limped slowly over to the half-door into the shed and looked at the four horses dozing away in the afternoon heat. Only Belle noticed him. She raised her elegant nearly white head and came to greet him at the door. Finn's eyes filled with tears. Angrily brushing them away, he turned his back on Belle and threw himself down on a mound of loose hay in the darkest corner of the barn.

"*You coulda got me one.*" That *was what Penny had said when Finn strapped himself in. Nothing more than that. Just, "You coulda got me one.*"

"*You coulda looked,*" *Finn answered.*

He took a deep personal satisfaction in speaking these days, now that his voice held firm most of the time. When it first began to change, it had sometimes alarmed him with its unpredictable ups and downs. Now he peered down through the little window of the plane at the tarmac racing faster and faster below. Even after more than a year of flying all over the country with his father, he still got a kick out of that.

Finn's father took up flying after he and his small computer company struck it rich four or five years ago. Finn was in sixth grade when they moved from the house he'd lived in all his life to the one they lived in now, in the suburbs. The new house had four big bedrooms instead of two, a large yard, and a three-car garage. His parents and Penny loved the new house, but Finn still missed the old one from time to time. When he and Penny were little, they had shared a bedroom, until his parents said he was big enough to move to a room the size of a closet in the attic. Finn loved that box of a room; it gave him his first sense of privacy and independence, though he liked being able to communicate with Penny through a crack in the floor.

Now he had a big room of his own, lined with

posters of his choice: Led Zeppelin; Cindy Crawford in a yellow bathing suit cut so high her thighs showed all the way to her waist and so low that her neckline plunged to her waist; a Reebok poster of Dee Brown dropping a slam dunk; and another red, white, and black one of The Doors, next to Aerosmith's album Pump, *looking like "something the cat dragged in," said his mother; several blown-up* National Geographic *photographs; and an old poster of the original* 101 Dalmatians *behind the door. Finn decided he wasn't quite ready to give that last one up yet. "Cool," said his friends when they saw the new room.*

These days his father was so busy he hardly had time to live in the new house. High school took more of Finn's own time, too. In a way that was okay—he liked high school, once he got over the shock, and he loved basketball. Even as a freshman he had been on the JV team, which kept him late at school. Now as a complete family they saw more of each other on holiday trips, like this long Memorial Day weekend, than they did during the rest of the year combined.

The Cessna 182 took off and mounted noisily into the sky. His father immediately turned to 270 degrees, toward West Thumb. The Absaroka Range loomed before and above them. To Finn it looked totally impassable, but he knew his father had pored over his maps, knew he was a careful, responsible pilot, and Finn had no doubt that he would find a way over the mountains. In the cockpit the noise intensified as the plane gained altitude.

The roar of a real engine jolted Finn out of his reverie. So focused had he been on walking through that last plane ride that it took him several seconds to recognize the barn at Riverview Farm and to remember he had come down here to be alone. The roaring engine was Gram's tractor coming in on the hayloft level above him. His grandmother came down the ladder.

"I wondered where you were," she said. "Julia's back. She came over to fetch those last bales. It's getting late and she has to be home for supper. Could you give us a hand?"

Finn felt her eyes seek his in the shadowy barn. He avoided them, wishing she wouldn't keep looking at him so intently. He wished she would make the worry lines around her mouth disappear along with the sadness in her eyes. He wished she would just cooperate with him, allow him to bury the whole thing, instead of wanting him to share it. Why would he want to *share* it? Didn't she realize he couldn't? Couldn't she see this was something only he had gone through? She couldn't possibly understand what it had been like. No one could. No one. Including him.

All he wanted now was . . . what? All he wanted now was—Finn got up from the mound of hay and met his grandmother's eyes—for her at least to *look* the way she used to, then he might be able to persuade himself that everything was basically all right, that this was just a bad patch, that it would clear up before too long.

But it was no use. Everything was basically all wrong. The truth was, his life had come to an end in the Absaroka Mountains. What was the point of walking through it? Why couldn't that doctor in Cody give him something to make him *forget*, instead of remember? Something to make him feel *good*, instead of bad?

"Coming?" asked his grandmother.

Reluctantly he started to climb up the ladder behind her to the loft, but his cast was too big for the rungs. Discouraged, he backed down and hobbled out the door and up the bank to the hayloft door, wishing he'd brought his crutch.

Julia didn't seem to expect anything from him when she greeted him in the hayloft. She was nearly fourteen, six months older than Penny and a year and a half younger than Finn. Her mother, Mylin, was a tiny, dark, beautiful Vietnamese woman; her father a robust, blond Vermonter named James. Julia was an uncanny mixture: dark blond hair, pitch-black eyes, a neat slim body that belied an impressive strength. Julia ran fast and jumped high, and she loved dancing as much as, or even more than, riding. Julia would dance for you at the drop of a hat. She and Penny had been best friends, but they had always included Finn in their never-ending projects and self-started adventures.

Clumsily, using only his left hand, Finn helped her unload the wagonful of hay, impressed again by the ease with which Julia handled the bales he pushed her way. Neither the heat nor the dust seemed to bother her a bit.

19

"Over there," was all she said from time to time, nodding to where she wanted to stack the next one.

That was Julia all over. Practical, matter-of-fact. Her slight body was no taller than a child's, and she still moved with the same supple coordination that he remembered. *It helps to be with someone who's the same as always,* Finn thought.

But when the last bale was in place and his grandmother went back up to the house, the barn was suddenly very silent. The heat in the loft was so thick that the hay dust hung motionless in the air. Julia looked at Finn and then down at the floor. From the lower level they heard Hiram stamp his foot, breaking the silence.

"Oh, Finn," she said.

Finn felt his heart shrink. He glared fiercely at the top of her bowed head. *Don't talk about it,* he warned her silently. *Don't mention Penny. Don't ask any questions. Don't say you're sorry, you don't know what sorry means. Don't . . .*

Julia raised her head and Finn saw that her face was streaked with dust and tears. Horrified, he started to back toward the door, but Julia stepped up to him. Standing on her toes, with one finger she touched his eyebrow where the scar passed through it. Then she turned and let herself down the ladder to feed the horses.

"That was dumb," she whispered to herself. "He can't handle anything like that. He's not himself right now."

She leaned against the foot of the ladder to collect herself. Julia knew she had less cause to mourn than

Gram or Finn; nonetheless, the terrible accident had been her first encounter with death. She still burst into tears often, even when she wasn't consciously thinking about the plane crash.

Yet, basically, Julia trusted life. Despite what had happened to Finn's family, despite what she saw on TV, for better or worse she believed with a certainty that she could never have put into words that in the largest possible sense, all would be well. Finn had, too, she knew. Even more than Penny, Finn had once trusted life.

Pushing herself off the ladder, she started down the main corridor of the barn toward the feed bins. It had gotten so dark that she had to feel her way, but passing the gate to the run-in shed she saw Belle's nose hanging over it and stopped to stroke it.

Julia was proud of Belle's filly Daisy, proud and determined to turn her into a successful show jumper; but it was Belle she loved the most. It was with Belle that she had won her first blue ribbon when she was six and had proudly added it to the string of blue, red, and yellow ribbons in the dusty tack room—ribbons won by Belle and Gram until both had retired last year, due to Belle's great age. And all her life it was to Belle she turned for comfort and advice, as though she were the aunt Julia did not have.

"What do you think, old lady? What can we do for Finn?" she asked, and then kissed the soft gray muzzle.

Out in the twilit pasture she saw the other horses grazing. As always, they clustered together, heads down, tearing at the short grass, cropping it closer and closer to the dry summer earth. Right near where they stood was a thick patch where the grass grew long and lush. But Julia knew they would not tread there. She didn't understand how they knew to avoid that rich green grass. Hiram and Horace were lent out to work, and Daisy was not even born when Ben, her handsome gray father, died two years ago.

Belle knew. Julia noticed that she often stood there, never grazing, but simply resting. Had she told the others it was Ben's grave? Or did some prehistoric instinct tell them that this was Belle's piece of turf, Belle's alone?

Whistling softly, Julia turned on the light and began her chores, amused and somehow cheered by the intricacies of the animal life in the barn. By the time she left, the other horses had joined Belle in the shed. Neither they nor she saw, at the far end of the pasture, a furtive figure making its way through the dark shadows at the edge of the pinewood.

A little while later, in the loft above, Finn heard the crunch of her bike tires on the dirt lane when she started home.

To the west of the pinewood, marked off from it by a crumbling stone wall, lay ten scrubby hilltop acres with a very old maple in the middle. It was a field that had once pastured Riverview Farm's heifers and now was overrun with black-eyed Susans, prickly wild strawberry vines, Indian paintbrush, and outcroppings of juniper—all signs of land let go to seed. As the sun began to sink at the close of this, the longest day of the year, the shadow of the old maple lengthened across the field and dark dropped like a blanket over the pinewood.

At nine o'clock, two figures came over the ridge at the top of the field. They passed through a line of trees and cut across the old pasture. When they got to the corner of the stone wall at the edge of the pinewood, they stopped.

"You sure you know what you're doing, Rafe?" asked Jack, his voice warbling between that of a man and a boy.

Rafe turned on him. "You want in or you want out?" he asked roughly.

Rafe was not tall, but he was powerfully built. His face had unexpected angles, and his brows met in the middle.

"Take it easy, Rafe. It's okay. You want the school trade, you got it."

"Where the hell is Pinky?"

"How would I know? Where are *we*?" Jack asked nervously. Born and raised in the town down on the river, he was about to be a junior in the high school. All his friends came from town, and although he worked on many neighborhood farms during haying season, he was not a country boy. The silent empty nightfall made him nervous.

Rafe paid no attention to him. He paced slowly alongside the wall, counting out loud. "Seven," he said and immediately disappeared. Had Jack not been close behind, he would have missed the gap entirely. Quickly he ducked and entered the wood where Rafe awaited him.

"C'mon, c'mon, kid—here's the way—you'll have to bend some." He shone a flashlight on the thick pines and, dodging and ducking their heads, they made their way to the clearing around the well.

Rafe squatted at the base of the springhouse, fingered some of the stones at its base, and then stood up, holding a small leather sack in his hand.

"That's some drop," said Jack. "Ain't nobody gonna find this place."

"Pinky showed it to me just once, in broad daylight. Otherwise I never could have found it again myself." Rafe's eyes narrowed. "Where the hell *is* he?"

"How'd Pinky ever find this place?" Jack asked.

Rafe pulled a cigarette from a pack in his pocket, offered it to Jack, drew another for himself, and lit both.

"Pinky was hunting last fall. Up there in the pasture his dog took off after a squirrel. He heard him ky-y-ing fit to kill in these woods. Called and called, but the dog wouldn't come, so finally Pinky had to go looking for him. Had a helluva time getting anywhere in here, but he finally found his dog. And when he saw that well, Pinky thought right off what to do with it. Gotta give him credit for that much."

A crackling noise made them both jump. The sound came from lower down the slope: twigs snapping, grunts, and finally stumbling footsteps.

Rafe snapped off the light and slipped his hand into the pocket of his jeans. Both held their breath. Just as Rafe started to withdraw his hand, a thin beam of light flicked over them and Pinky emerged on all fours. His face was greasy with sweat and covered with bits of dead twigs and pine needles.

When he reached the clearing, he stood up and said, "Surprised you, didn't I? Thought you guys would never get here."

"You goddam fool, Pinky, I might've blown your head off." Rafe's lips were drawn back with rage, and he started forward, one hand still in his pocket, the other balled into a fist. Pinky fell back a step, scraping his back against the encircling wall of dead boughs. His sallow, doughy face gleamed white under the filth, and his reddish hair clung to his scalp in frail, girlish curls.

He held his arm up as if to protect his face. "Jeez, Rafe, what the hell's biting you? Look what I done—I found a new way to the drop. Must've been the way to the old well from the house. It's grown over so bad, nobody else would ever find it. Might come in handy some day."

"Anybody see you down there, you damn fool?"

"Hell, no, Rafe, who you think I am? The sun was down already." Pinky was pulling himself together. "Hey, who found this place, anyways?" He swaggered to the stone well, looked Jack up and down, and said, "Well, kid, how ya like bein' in the fast lane? Pretty cool, huh?"

Rafe snickered. "Some fast lane. Biggest threat we got here's some old woman lives alone down there." He drew deeply on his cigarette.

"'Cept she don't live alone no more," said Pinky. He winked at Jack. "I seen that grandson of hers limpin' to the barn this afternoon. Seems he's come to live with her 'cause his folks got killed in a plane crash. The whole town's talking about it."

Jack turned to Rafe. "I know that kid, Rafe. Him and his sister used to visit the old lady every summer during first cut. I seen him when I helped out. I'm half a year older'n him, but I gotta tell you, Rafe, he's gonna be in my class at school, 'case that makes any difference."

"Knock it off—that has nothin' to do with us," said Rafe. "Just stay clear of him, the two of you. Okay, let's make sure we got our stories straight. Jack, what's the routine?"

"There'll be a bag here every Thursday, delivered sometime the night before, so's we don't cross. One of us gotta pick it up at ten o'clock Thursday night, divvy it up, and leave the dough from the week before. We rotate, one by one. Nobody knows who picks up the dough and brings the next stash, and nobody knows exactly when. All we gotta do is pick it up Thursday night."

Pinky, watching Rafe's face, suddenly knew, with the crafty certainty of suspicious minds, that Rafe knew who picked up the cash. In fact—Pinky's mind whizzed faster than his reason—*Rafe* picked it up. Or at least gave the orders. Could that be true? Could Rafe have something going on behind their backs? *By God, I bet he does,* thought Pinky, and he tucked the thought away to use another time.

"Okay," said Rafe. "Now let's get out of here. Pinky, I'll give you a lift back to your truck. C'mon, kid, this way." And he started back up the path toward the field.

When they emerged he told Jack, "Just remember: It's seven paces in from that corner. That's the way in for us. Yeah, yeah, Pinky—we ever need two ways to unload dope, I'll come to you for help." Rafe gave a snort of laughter. "Them feds hangin' out in town . . . think they're on to us." He looked at the thick wall of trees behind them. "Ain't a cop in the state gonna find this place."

The three cut diagonally across the pasture to where Rafe had left his truck. The engine started, and the truck bounced slowly through a copse of trees to the road. No one in the world knew they had been there. No one except Toq. He wrinkled his nose at the stink of cigarette smoke and turned back to his den deep in the pinewood.

Chapter 2

As day succeeded day, Finn decided he now lived in some strange new dimension. No matter how long and affectionate his connection to Riverview Farm, neither he nor his life here now bore any resemblance to the past. Gone was that life, gone his parents, gone his sister. And, as well, gone was the self he had once felt so comfortable with, hidden by walls he had built for protection.

The only way he managed to get through each day was to treat it like a task he must perform, a little like walking a tightrope carrying a heavy burden. To stay in control from one end to the other, without losing his balance and falling to the darkness below, was all he asked. One more day over.

Establishing a fixed routine helped: up at six, breakfast, chores, and, almost always, the appearance of Julia around noon, by which time she would have spent two hours working out at the barre in her family's barn, finished her half-day baby-sitting job, and be ready to work with Daisy. When Julia came, it helped move the day along.

For the first week she never mentioned Penny or his parents or the accident, but simply went about her chores as though nothing were more important than shoveling manure out of the shed or brushing Belle or feeding the hens. Sometimes she spoke of the dancing camp she was going to for a week later in the summer, and this made Finn uneasy. He didn't want to hear about her going away, even for a week, though he never would have said so, even if he could talk.

Then one day, as he watched her cleaning Daisy's hooves, she said casually, "You know, you really ought to try riding again. I bet Gram would let you take Belle out, if we went easy, and I could ride old Hiram. I'd help you mount."

His tightrope teetered back and forth. Julia looked up and saw that his face had closed down and dropped the subject.

Finn was relieved, but he envied her. He envied her pleasure in the moment. The sound of her voice as she chatted her thoughts aloud was like background music, light and undemanding, yet with an undercurrent of joy.

Yes, Julia definitely helped move the days along.

The nights, however, remained a torment, and he came to dread dragging himself up the stairs to bed, only to fight off the nightmares that appeared with the dark. To deal with them, he turned his ramparts of defense into an imaginary fort, staffed with soldiers under his command. Unlike the springhouse, this fort had very high walls upon which he stood guard even when exhaustion overcame him and finally, fitfully, his body slept. But his mind flew into action at the approach of a dream, first rousing him to wakefulness and then banishing the dream from his memory. At such times he found himself staring into the darkness with his heart racing so hard that he figured the noise of it was what woke him. Once he imagined he heard animals crying in the woods.

On bad nights nothing on earth could have persuaded him to go back to sleep. Instead, he pulled his mattress to the window and lay staring out at the stars, willing himself to count every one.

Then one evening at the end of his second week at the farm, when he was alone in the kitchen, he opened the drawer under the telephone and saw his mother's old recorder. Immediately pain sliced through him and he slammed the drawer shut.

Too late. She appeared in the kitchen. He could *feel* her standing next to him. He smelled her smell—a comfortable oily smell that hung about her for days when she worked on a portrait. His mother? Here? Could it be?

Caught by surprise, *"Mom!"* started in his chest, rose swelling into his throat, and wedged there. When he heard the ugly gargling sound he made, Finn fled the kitchen.

But the next day he opened the drawer again and

deliberately stared at the recorder, waiting for his mother to appear. When she did not, he let out his breath. *Fool*, he said to himself. He took the recorder into his good hand and curled his fingers around the smooth wood, unable not to remember the melodies she had taught him to play over the years.

That night, rather than trying to count the stars, he took out the recorder and sat crouched in the window playing very soft music to them. The fingers of his right hand were stiff in their glove, but to his amazement it worked. He could play, and the music seemed to soften his tight swollen chest. It filtered through the cork that blocked his throat and filled his fort with something approaching peace, so that he climbed into his bed and dared to close his eyes. After that he began to sleep in fits and starts.

Waking up had its own traps. He had to get out of bed immediately; otherwise, no matter how high and tight he built his inner fortress, no matter how craftily he suppressed his dreams, the pain would seep through the walls as he woke. Speed was what mattered now. If he was fast enough to rise the moment his eyes opened, if he took off his cast and stumbled hastily into the shower, he might keep enough balance to get through another day.

Breakfast wasn't too bad. Gram had given up her stream of words. She no longer searched his face for signs of recovery, but simply peeled an orange and sipped her tea and commented occasionally on matters at hand.

— ♠ —

Two weeks after Finn had arrived at Riverview Farm, Julia said, "Tomorrow's the Fourth of July already. I can't believe how fast time flies."

Finn had been peeling potatoes for Gram. He had learned to do that despite the glove, though his left hand wielded the knife awkwardly. He put it down and looked at Julia in disbelief. *Time flies?*

"Are you and your family going to the parade?" asked Gram.

"Oh, gosh, yes," said Julia. "We've never missed the parade. You know that. Dad's driving the fire truck this year and . . ."

Finn stopped listening and picked up the knife again and focused on the potato in his gloved right hand. If he could pare it left-handed in one piece without breaking the peel, there would be no nightmare tonight. Yup. He made it. Good omen, that. He was still in control.

"How about it, Finny? Shall we go for a while?"

Finn, at the sound of his name, looked up to find his grandmother smiling at him.

"We're all going to the parade—want to come? You remember what fun it is," Julia now said.

Finn stared at them both. Were they crazy? Didn't they get the picture yet? The parade was *way* out-of-bounds. How could they ask this of him? An enormous "*No*" rose to his throat. Couldn't they hear it? He shook his head furiously.

Julia shrugged. "Have it your way," she said. Her small neat face closed in irritation. "I'll go with my family."

That day she rode off bareback on old Hiram and didn't return until the shadows of the maples stretched all the way to the goat pasture. Finn went to the door when he heard her come up from the barn, but she mounted her bicycle without looking at him and pedaled off down the lane.

Two mornings later Gram said, "I'd like you to weed the vegetable garden for me, please, Finny. I haven't touched it since we got back from Cody."

Julia had not appeared at all on the Fourth of July, and Finn did not want even to imagine what that meant. Instead, he concentrated on the task before him. The work was demanding enough to keep his mind as busy as his body. As he started to weed he noticed that his good hand had lost its hospital pallor; the long narrow fingers were brown, the muscles of his left arm looked as taut as when he played basketball—even the nails of that hand had grown long enough to cut.

It had taken him several tries before he worked out how to keep weight off his left leg without leaning on his right hand. The doctor had told him he must wear the right-hand glove until the burn scar had toughened and to use that hand sparingly, so he troweled and dug with his awkward left hand, collecting small piles of weeds that he then scooped up to drop in a canvas bag.

His legs bothered him more. The left one hurt from his groin to his foot, and the cast on the ankle kept getting in his way. This frustrated him at times, but he had to admit to himself that he found a certain comfort in wearing the cast and using the crutch. They were good excuses for his self-imposed solitude.

By midday the garden was about done. Finn swore to himself that he was not listening for her, but when he heard Julia's bike coming up the lane, he pulled himself to his feet and dragged the weed bag to the garden gate.

"Hi," said Julia, as he stumped into the kitchen. Her face was as open as usual, her voice as fresh. Finn felt light-headed with relief.

Julia flopped into her usual chair. "That was a *great* Fourth," she said. "Lefty Thompson won the greased pole contest, and Mom got a first prize for her peonies. And the fireworks! You're just too far away to have seen them, but they were fantastic. I love the ones that whir."

Finn forced himself to listen.

"Things are really popping downtown," Julia said, more to Gram than to Finn. "Did you know there are real live *narcs* there now? Apparently they arrived sometime last week. You should have heard everybody talking about it after the parade."

"So someone told me, but I didn't pay much attention. It's hard to believe the federal government would spend a lot of time and money on drug trafficking in this corner of the world." Finn's grandmother poured herself a fresh cup of tea.

"But it's true, Gram," said Julia. "There really is an honest-to-goodness ring, and gangs—even at school, I know kids involved. Well, to tell the truth, I don't really know them, I just know about them . . . Anyway, here's some more news: Did you all hear the coyotes last night?"

"I'll say I did," said Gram. "They were at it from about two to four, I figure, yipping and yowling back and forth, one pack to another."

"Well, they got one of the Thompsons' lambs. Killed it right under the fence. How's that for hard news!"

Coyotes! Finn felt the curly hairs on the nape of his neck prickle and lift. The last time he'd run into coyotes they were waiting patiently for him to die, and when he didn't they ate— He slammed the image down before it formed.

"They didn't used to come this near the house when old Mick was alive," Gram was saying.

"Well, now, you see! I've been telling you and telling you it's time you got another dog," said Julia. She grinned and made the thumbs-up sign. "Mom said they sounded as though they were right in your pinewood last night."

But, coyotes, here at the farm? How could he have slept through that? Or had he? Was that what he'd heard? Finn clenched his good hand.

"Maybe so, but I think that's where that big animal lives."

"You mean the one you told me about? A couple of other people on the hill have seen it, too," Julia said. "In fact, Dad said it crossed right in front of the pickup on his way home from work last month. Dad thinks it's some kind of hybrid, like a coydog or even a wolf cross. Too big for a coyote, he says."

"Oh, everyone around here talks about coydogs," said Finn's grandmother impatiently. "They can happen, but they're not really a breed. Still, I don't know what else to call that one. He *looked* more like a wolf, the two or three times I've seen him over the years, but wolf hybrids are really rare around here, or anywhere for that matter. As for killing lambs, all I know is a dog gone bad kills for the sake of killing and a coyote will only kill what it needs and come back to finish the carcass when it's hungry. Hybrids, I don't know." She frowned. "In any case, nobody better mess with my barnyard."

Finn leaned forward, with his elbows on his knees. This other animal they were talking about, could it be? Could it be the same one he had seen three summers ago, when he was twelve? That was no coyote.

He listened carefully as his grandmother and Julia continued to compare notes on what they'd heard about the big fellow. A vivid picture filled Finn's mind: On his way across the hay meadow to help load bales, a large wolflike animal had trotted across the horses' pasture toward the pinewood. Even then Finn could tell by the way it moved and the way it carried its tail that it was not a coyote. Not a regular dog, either. It stopped when it saw Finn and stared straight at him, and he felt something like awe. Then it moved on and into the pinewood. He'd never seen it since. *Hey, wouldn't it be great if it still lived nearby?* The possibility roused him. *That would be cool. I'll keep my eye out*, he thought, and found that he wanted to smile.

"That reminds me, Julia," he heard his grandmother say. "You and Finn better check to be sure the goats' electric fence wire is turned on. That nanny Clara is due next week. Coyotes love newborns—or anything else they can take without danger for that matter. And as for that other one, whatever he is, I wouldn't trust him not to kill a full-grown goat. Well"—she pushed her plate aside—"anyone want seconds on the tuna? . . . You sure? I got some ice-cream sandwiches, if you want . . . Popsicles, too."

Julia went to the freezer, got out a couple of Popsicles, and tossed one to Finn. He caught it with his right hand, surprised that the gloved fingers had moved almost as nimbly as before.

"Good catch," she said, and he did smile. "Come on down to the barn with me."

Finn looked down to unwrap the Popsicle. It was root beer.

"Hey, Finny, we don't have time to waste. Forget the root beer." That was his father's voice. Right there in the kitchen. Couldn't the others hear it, too?

He was so tall and the inside of the airport freezer was so deep that he could bury himself in it up to his waist. The cold smelled like a chemical and miniature icicles formed on his eyebrows and inside his nose as his fingers scrabbled around among the frosty white Popsicles and ice-cream cups. From far away he heard his father's voice over the hum of the freezing unit.

". . . weather coming in . . ."

Hey, what do you know? Finn thought as he spied the familiar wrapper. A genuine root beer *Popsicle! And his fingers closed around the prize.*

"Finn!"

"Hey. Come on, Finn, don't be a drag. I need you to hold Daisy while I put a saddle on her for the first time, and anyway I can't remember where the fence battery is."

When he didn't rise, she reached down and pulled on the back of his T-shirt.

"Hey. Earth to Finn. Earth to Finn. Come *on.*"

Feeling as hollow as when he'd left the hospital, Finn rose clumsily to his feet and followed her out the door. On his way past the garbage can he lifted the lid and dropped the untouched Popsicle in.

Five days later, at six-thirty in the morning, Finn's grandmother called Julia and told her Clara had just had twins. Half an hour later Julia leaned over the gate and watched fascinated as Clara licked and nuzzled her new kids. The whole community in the barn seemed affected by the birth. Monica had moved her observation post from her usual beam to one directly over the goat pen; all four horses hung their heads over the gate; even the busy, clucking hens were quiet; and the two young wethers—nephews of Clara, named Donder and Blitzen—lay at a respectful distance from the new mother.

"They're a fine pair," Julia breathed. "And you're a fine mother, Clara. I knew you'd take to it right away. Now stop worrying; they'll be up in no time," she added, as Clara cleaned off the last of the afterbirth and started to nudge first one kid and then the other to her feet. The newborns were both female. They looked like tiny replicas of their mother with her fawn coloring and the same droopy ears.

Julia thought back to the first time she had seen a newborn animal: It was Belle's first foal, born when Julia was eight. She remembered tiptoeing into the barn at dawn and peeking through the slatted gate of the foaling stall, and there it lay—a bay colt. What a nervous new mother Belle had been.

Julia smiled, remembering the dignified gray mare losing her composure: Her nostrils flared and her eyes were wide with wonder as she gazed at the foal lying in the straw—that long-legged, big-headed creature, covered with mucus and utterly helpless. To Julia, even at eight, it seemed as though Belle looked at him in fear and trembling, and for the first time it sank in that this creature had come from inside Belle's own body, just as someday a child might form in her own. There he was, in the flesh, and it was up to Belle and Belle alone to raise him up and set him free. Then suddenly Belle's fear had given way to a surge of exultation, and she had stepped out of the shed into the breaking day and trumpeted at the top of her lungs, again and again, as though announcing to the whole valley, *"He's here! He's Here! He's here!"*

Well, well, imagine remembering all that, Julia mused and turned her attention back to the twin kids.

"What shall we call them?" she asked Clara.

She looked past the two young wethers lying in the doorway. It was another hot day, but the goats' pasture was still fresh and green. Patches of white clover and purple vetch sprinkled the dewy grass.

"How about Clover and Vetch? Okay?" Julia turned around and addressed the barn. "Did you hear that, everybody? Clara's new kids are called Clover and Vetch."

Suddenly a raucous and triumphant cackle burst from the hens' quarters. It went on and on, louder and louder, all the other hens joining in, cheering, arguing, exhorting one another to see who could celebrate the loudest. Julia laughed.

"Maybe they're jealous. You might think that old hen had invented the sun and the moon all by herself," she said to the new mother. "Although I suppose it must be sort of cool to lay an egg."

Pausing to collect the warm egg, Julia left the barn and started to jog up to the house. She was pretty sure this new Finn would not have gone down to see the twins on his own and it made her feel both sad and impatient with him. He'd *love* those kids. Rounding the corner of the house, she saw him at the edge of the vegetable garden. His back was to her, and he was standing motionless, staring out into the meadow.

"Finn!" she started to call, but in the nick of time

the word stuck in her throat. There, not a hundred yards away, stood the strange hybrid animal. He was a few paces from the edge of the pinewood. His rich coat gleamed in the sunlight, he held his bushy tail at half-mast, and the deep hazel eyes gazed unblinking at Finn. Julia halted in midstride, but the animal had seen her. In a fluid unhurried motion, he resumed his track to the wood and disappeared without a trace.

Julia burst into the kitchen ahead of Finn.

"Did you see him?" she called.

Finn's grandmother was drying dishes and putting them on shelves.

"See who?" she asked.

"That—that—that wolf-dog—or whatever he is," Julia exclaimed as Finn hobbled fast through the door after her. His face was flushed and he panted from haste. "He was right in the field just now when I came up the lane. Finn was in the garden—he saw him, didn't you, Finn?"

He nodded.

"I saw you and him staring at each other. He's awesome. You wouldn't believe the way he and Finn sized each other up, Gram. Maybe we'll see him more often, now the hay is down."

"What's that animal doing out in the middle of the field in broad daylight right after Clara's twins were born?" Finn's grandmother asked sharply. "I don't like the sound of this."

"Well, the fence is on, so they're safe, anyway. By

the way, I sort of named them already: Clover and Vetch. Okay with you?"

Gram's face was grim, but she nodded.

"Fine by me, but that fence better do its job . . . You kids want eggs for breakfast?"

"I can't stay—I just came to see the twins. I have to be home by nine-thirty. Mom wants me to go to town with her. You need anything from the Grand Union?" Julia asked Gram.

"No, thanks, Julia dear, but you might think about getting some bug spray for Daisy. The flies really get to her and she'd probably give you a smoother ride, when you start getting on her."

"Yes'm. Will you mind spraying her when I'm gone at camp, Finny?"

Finn nodded and Julia did a little pirouette on one sneakered toe.

"Thank you, kind sir," she said. "Now, let's go see the babies. Come on, Finn—I insist."

Awkwardly, feeling self-conscious and out of place, Finn lowered himself clumsily down beside Julia and took one of the twins onto his lap. He had not been prepared for the effect the newborns had on him. At first sight his heart felt as though it had turned to soup. They were irresistible. He held the toylike creature to his face and buried his nose in its sweet-smelling goaty hide.

Julia, noticing, waited a while and then handed him the other twin.

"Here, you take this one, too. I've got to clean the

shed and it's nearly eight. It's okay, Clara," she added, as the doe moved protectively toward Finn. "He'll take good care of them."

Inch by inch Finn's body started to relax. The twins fell asleep in his arms and he leaned carefully back against the wall and held them, unmoving. Only his chest moved up and down with each breath, the two sleeping toys rising and falling with it. The faint sounds of Julia working in the shed faded away. His mind was blank.

A familiar smell filtered through his trance. Without warning it had seeped into his nostrils and permeated every pore of his body. Straw. Grain. Then the musty smell of the goats, and somewhere behind him, horse, chicken, hay, dust. The smells merged into a familiar cloud of memory and affection. The barn. The farm. Summer. How good it all smelled.

Suddenly he felt Julia beside him again. Startled, he sat forward and the kids tumbled off his chest and staggered over to their anxious mother, who nudged them to her udder.

"How Penny would have loved them," Julia breathed. "She always—" Her voice broke and she started to cry.

Finn drew away from her and a scowl as black as a storm cloud closed his face.

Seeing it, Julia burst out, "Oh, for God's sake, Finn! You're not the only one hurting around here. Look at Gram. Look at *me!*" Her voice was rough and blurred and the tears poured unchecked down her cheeks. "She was my best friend, you know. You think *I* don't miss her? That I don't hurt every day, too? You can't live your whole life like some—some"—she hiccoughed with grief—"some sort of *crab*." She turned and flung herself out of the barn.

Finn stood at the gate to the goat shed, staring at the twins, who had tired of nursing and lay curled one against the other in the straw. The barn was utterly still.

She's right, he thought.

Ever so slightly his burden shifted, threatening his balance. A chink appeared in his armor, allowing in a ray of light. When it did, Finn started to panic. Anxiety billowed, but he shut it down. *No.*

No feelings. No sweet baby goats. Just stay sightless, deaf, numb inside and out.

No, not quite numb inside. Not numb enough. Inside, terrifying emotions swirled and stormed. His hands clenched the iron gate, the wounded one sending warning stabs of pain. He clenched the gate harder, wanting the pain to keep his mind busy.

They all seem to want me to let these horrors out and pass them around, like some kind of offering. NO! I must not, I must not do that. If I keep my balance day by day, I'll be safe, in control. Julia nearly robbed me of that control just now. It's simply a matter of control, that's all. I know what I'm doing, I'm doing just fine.

A swallow swooped through the low-ceilinged barn and startled him. He dragged his good fingers fiercely through his hair and started for the sunlit door. Passing the horse shed, he saw Belle at the gate, and he paused. *It's okay, old lady,* he told her soundlessly. *I'm okay.*

Then he turned his back on her and left the barn.

Down in the town Julia and her mother came out of the Grand Union just as a gangling boy walked in.

"Well, hey, Jack," said Julia.

"Hey." Jack stood awkwardly at the entrance, the door held open by the electric eye.

"Mom, you remember Jack—he helped bale the hay over at Riverview. He'll be in Finn's class this fall."

Mylin Hatch nodded. "How's your mom, Jack?"

"Okay, thanks, Mrs. Hatch."

A pale, redheaded, older man approached them. He stopped in the doorway and greeted Jack. Julia half turned to the stranger, expecting Jack to introduce them, but Jack pushed him through the entrance into the store and the door sighed shut behind them.

"Jeezus!" Jack hissed furiously at Pinky. "What the hell you think you're doing, coming up to me like that?

"Well *excuse* me for breathing, you little punk. Why the hell shouldn't I say hello to you or anyone else? After all, I live here, too, you know."

"You fat ass, then why don't you even know that's the girl lives right near the old lady at Riverview Farm—practically lives *at* Riverview Farm? Kee-*rist,* I'm of half a mind to tell Rafe she seen you talkin' to me."

"You mind your tongue, kid. I got some ideas of my own about our friend Rafe. You keep your mouth shut, I may just tell you what they are."

— ✦ —

About a week after the twins were born Finn came downstairs one morning to find his grandmother stewing over her farm bills. When she had pushed the last of the papers aside, she looked up at Finn and said, "Well, Finny, I don't have any jobs for you this afternoon, so you better get started on the summer reading list the high school mailed us. Time is marching on."

Finn's perpetual frown deepened.

"It's no use looking like that. I know you dread the whole idea of school, and I don't blame you, but you can't just drop out now. You're not yet sixteen. It's just another one of those things you've got to accept. As for the reading list, with Julia off to camp next month you'll find time heavy on your hands, so you may as well get in the habit now."

When Finn swiveled around and stared out the window, Gram went on deliberately. "That therapist the Cody doctor recommended to us will be back the end of August. You'll be having regular appointments with him that should help you talk again. And once you talk, Finny—I mean talk about the crash, talk your way through it, the way he said—when you get it all out in the open, I'm sure as sure can be that—"

But Finn swung out of his chair, grabbed his crutch, and fled.

"Walk *through it, stupid*," he wanted to shout at Gram as he stumbled out of the kitchen. *He said to walk my way through it.*

He pulled himself up the stairs to the attic and fell

onto his bed. *All right, all right, all right,* he would lift the drawbridge to his fort and let the memories in.

"Flight Service said 'chance of thunderstorms' in this front we're headed into, but it looks okay so far," Finn's father shouted over the roar of the engine. *"I figured we'd take a look—if we see trouble, we can turn around and head back."*

Finn looked down. They were at the highest point of their flight. Mountains lay below and around them. Had his father not grown up in Wyoming, right next to the Absarokas, had he not hunted wild sheep in the wildest sections of these mountains all his life, Finn might have been afraid. By a long shot this was the most remote course they had ever flown. The plane had shuddered and strained to reach the altitude his father needed to wind his way through the range.

The sky, gray when they left the little airport, now darkened rapidly. Although the ceiling of clouds was still above them, the air seemed suddenly harder to see through.

Finn's mother leaned forward in her seat and called, "What do you think, Neil? Maybe we should go back."

"Damn. I just don't know; maybe you're right, honey. Let's take a look."

He banked the plane north over the tip of a mountain and ran head on into a wall of weather.

"Not a good idea. Okay, we'll play it safe and head back."

But when Finn's father wheeled the Cessna to the

east, they found themselves surrounded by the front. The ceiling had dropped. Clouds loomed on every side, dark ominous clouds. Suddenly a flash turned them a livid greenish yellow. The plane staggered.

"Oh, Lord, no," Finn's father breathed.

He jerked the wheel hard to the right as turbulence hit again, hurling them first up and then down. A peak slid past them on their left, only slightly lower than the wing. The plane bucked hard again. Rain spattered the windshield. Lightning flashed.

"Oh, sweet Lord in heaven, no . . ."

Again the plane bucked. It lurched sideways, reared again, and then dropped sickeningly. Finn heard Penny cry out. He felt his own throat tighten over a shout of fear.

"Unlock your door," Finn's father yelled as the plane leveled out. He let go of the wheel with one hand long enough to unlock his own.

Finn found the latch to his door and pushed it. His fingers trembled and his body felt like ice. He remembered what his father had told them the first time he took the family up in the plane: "If we ever get in bad trouble, make sure we have a way out." Now he looked down. A way out? Out where? He could see no land at all, only swirling gray and streaks of rain and, once again, a lurid flash of lightning. A clap of thunder drowned out the engine.

"Dad!" Finn shouted.

But Finn's father was wrestling with the wheel to make the Cessna rise. Sweat ran down his face.

Buffeted on every side, yawing wildly, like a creature drowning in the sea, the little plane struggled for the surface of the storm. Inch by inch it rose. Finn could feel the ascent in the seat of his pants and a wash of hope warmed his icy body. His father would get them out of this.

Then everything happened at once. Gray turned to black. A bolt of lightning shot over the right wing. The plane hit a solid wall of turbulence and staggered, sending shock waves through the fuselage until Finn was sure it would break apart. His father cried out as the wheel jerked free of his hands. Immediately the plane heaved convulsively to the left. And then it dropped . . . down . . . down . . . The left wing rose when the Cessna hit the bottom of the air pocket. Finn's father wrenched the wheel, but it was too late. With an earsplitting crash the wing hit the side of a mountain. The plane swung against the rock face and slid crazily from ledge to ledge. Down, down, down they fell, until a boulder spun the Cessna to a standstill on its side. Flames sprang from the engine. Smoke filled the cabin. Finn's door flew open. Instinctively he unlocked his belt and fell out of the burning tilted plane.

Finn could not continue. Shaking all over, sick to his stomach, dragging for breath, he got up from the edge of his bed and, forgetting his ankle, started toward the window for air. His leg buckled under him and he fell to the floor.

"Finn?" his grandmother called from below. "Finn, are you all right?"

All right? he hissed to himself. *All right? I'll never be all right again. Nothing will ever be all right again, I don't care what that doctor in Cody said. I cannot walk through it. I will not walk through it. Not ever again, no matter what they say.*

But even as he raged, his heart was filled with grief. Somewhere there was a place he had once known and could not find again. Sometimes, as he sat in his window at night, he would think about this place Someone he knew lived there, but he didn't know who. He had no idea where or what that place might be or who he would find there, though the memory of it haunted him like a piece of music he could not name or finish. All he knew for sure was that that place once existed and he had lost the way into it. But if to find it meant reliving his agony in the Absarokas—No, he could not bear it. There must be another way.

Chapter 3

As one hot July day followed another, farmers who had rejoiced in the perfect haying weather in June began to search the sky anxiously for signs of the rain needed to grow a second crop. The wildlife in the pinewood felt the effects of the drought as well. Prey was harder to find. Even the smallest creatures hid from the heat of day, thereby forcing the larger ones to hunt farther afield.

Late one night the four coyotes in the pinewood lay panting on the thick bed of needles. A quarter-moon cast little light in a sky hazed over with heat. Riverview Farm was barely visible, even to the keen-eyed animals whose gaze never left it. Triangular ears erect, scruffy gray coats merged with shadow, they lay—mother, father, and two adolescent males—with the telltale yellow eyes of their breed fixed on the barn at the foot of the long horse pasture.

From time to time one or the other of the young ones rose, trembling slightly, and pointed toward the farmyard like an arrow straining at the bow. Saliva hung in ropes from the chops of both. Ever since watching their father bring down a neighborhood lamb, they had throbbed with restlessness to make their first kill. Especially now, with the lengthening drought and the dearth of game, each had but one aim in mind: a full belly.

With a muffled whine, the mother coyote yawned hungrily. Taking it as a signal, the larger brother rose to his feet and took a step forward. Immediately the father uttered a low growl and his son sank obediently to his belly, nose still pointed at the nearly invisible farm.

The smaller coyote was tawnier than his brother. His coat looked cream-colored in the dim light. He crouched, humpbacked and tense.

Deep in the wood behind them, Toq watched the scene. He knew about the birth of the kids—a vision of them flashed into his mind now, stirring his own hunger. Suddenly Toq stiffened and the hackles along his spine lifted. From somewhere north of the coyotes' den, he heard something moving along the edge of the pines.

The father coyote, too, heard the sound.

Man!

Twigs snapped sharply. Some man was trying to enter the wood from the field above. A thin beam of light pierced the web of trunks and branches. It bobbed here and there as though trying to find a way in. Finally the light withdrew. The sound of footsteps dwindled. Whoever it was had given up and returned to the pasture above the wood. The father coyote turned three times and lay down near the mouth of the den to doze away the rest of the night, and Toq crept back to his lair.

Pinky cursed all the way across the old heifer pasture. He swore softly and viciously, using every foul word he knew. His breath sounded like a whistle in his throat, his nose ran, and his hands shook so hard that he jammed them in the pockets of his overalls.

"God, if I knew it was gonna be like this, I never would have tried the stuff," he moaned to himself.

Pinky was newly addicted to cocaine. For the past few weeks his sole interest in the drug ring that Rafe had organized in the town was having access to the magical, enchanting, deadly powder. He knew he couldn't ask Rafe for dope, even though it was *his* dog that had discovered the abandoned well, *his* suggestion to use it for a drop, *his* idea to bring Jack in, and even though he suspected that Rafe was into some double-dealing of his own.

When Pinky joined the ring four months earlier, he was clean but greedy; all he wanted was to earn enough money to buy a new car. But now, now all he wanted was to get high and stay high; and in between, it was agony. This was Wednesday, and it was Jack's week on, which gave Pinky twenty-four hours to pinch the stash and cut it with junk, *if he could just remember how to get at it*. He was sober the first time he found that well, sober the three times he'd been on duty to make the drop and take the money. But now, his head whirled and his stomach heaved. Now, he couldn't remember which corner to start from. And was it six paces in? Seven?

He halted under the old maple in the middle of the pasture, determined to start again. But the night was too dark. No matter how hard he tried, Pinky could not remember the way into that pinewood.

"I'll wait until dawn," he said aloud. "Then I'll be able to see. Then, by God, I'll find it."

He began to shake so hard that he had to sit down. At the thought of having to wait all that time for a snort, Pinky felt a wave of nausea.

His face crumpled and his voice broke, "Oh, God, help me—I am losing my mind."

The following week was hotter than ever. Instead of inching its way up into a pastel sky, the sun appeared whole each day out of the haze and hung motionless over the river valley. In the barn Clara's twins were undaunted by the heat. They suckled and gamboled by turns, trying the patience of Donder and Blitzen, who nonetheless put up with them. Cosseted by animals and humans alike, they were the darlings of Riverview Farm. Already, in just two weeks, they had assumed distinct personalities: Clover was shy and more delicate than her twin; she demanded less attention and received more. On the other hand, whether butting Clara or bleating at anyone who looked her way, Vetch was a scamp. It was she who, at three days old, tried to poke her nose through the fence dividing the goats from the horses and got the shock of her life from the wire. Clover watched and never went near it.

Up at the house Finn sat in the rocker by the kitchen window, reading *Catcher in the Rye* and fingering his face where the stitches had been removed. Because of the heat he had risen earlier than usual— even before his grandmother—and only took up the book to keep his thoughts at bay. His first look at it had convinced him that this was not for him; but as he forced himself to continue, he found to his surprise that Holden Caulfield's story appealed to him, and he decided that he would make time to read it this summer.

Gram sat at the kitchen table writing letters. At one point she put down her pen and said to Finn, "Maybe you and Julia should go for a swim this afternoon. It's too hot to ride."

Finn continued to stare at the book, but his mind jumped to the swimming hole at the river, where the three of them—he, Julia and Penny—used to go all the time. There was a rope tied to a thick branch that dangled over the river's edge; they would take turns with the other kids in the neighborhood, swinging on the rope as far out over the river as they could before letting go and plunging in. Finn always jumped the farthest. How great it felt—his body arching through the air. In his mind's eye he saw the grin of delight splitting his face. Yes, it was fun. But there'd be a ton of kids there today in this heat. *No . . . No . . .* He shook his head and went on reading.

Even Julia was affected by the heavy, humid day and decided not to work with Daisy. She got Finn to hold the filly while she hosed her down. Daisy was outraged, which made even Finn laugh soundlessly. Afterward they turned the hose on each other, but by the time they got back to the house their shirts were nearly dry and their heavy wet jeans only made them hotter than ever. Finn thought his gloved hand and plastered foot would melt.

Later on, sitting in the shade of the largest maple on the lawn, Gram finished her iced tea and said, "Just look at those horses out there. Have you ever noticed how Belle sometimes stands on Ben's grave half-asleep? The others won't set foot there and even Belle won't eat that thick green grass."

Julia smiled. "I sure have. I know it sounds kind of mushy, but every time I see her there, I'm sure she's dreaming of old Ben."

"They certainly were devoted—and my, oh my, what a handsome pair they made. I'm glad Daisy was on the way before Ben died, even though she came as something of a surprise. She's going to make a fine horse for you, Julia. Well"—she got to her feet and collected their three glasses—"I say let's treat ourselves to a video tonight. Come with me to choose one, Julia, and I'll drive you home afterward."

And so the day faded into night, slowly, hotly.

When Finn went to bed the attic room was so stuffy that he pulled his mattress right off to the open window and lay down with the recorder. At first glance the sky was absolutely black, blanketed by the haze of heat; Finn could see no light other than Venus. But as his eyes adjusted to the night, he was able to make out shapes in the landscape—the barn, the great maples, even the fence line of the goat pasture—and as his vision cleared pinpoints of light showed in the sky behind the murk.

I'll play to them, he thought. *In another hour the heat will rise and then I'll play to the stars.*

But the long, hot day had been too much for all his sentinels; they slumped on the ramparts of his fort, and Finn fell sound asleep.

In the pinewood, the father coyote gave a signal. The two younger ones slunk soundlessly into the horse pasture and crossed it at an angle that brought them to the fence near the barn. There they sank down to their elbows and haunches. Ears pricked, yellow eyes half-closed, jaws barely ajar, they lay motionless as though listening to the night. Nothing stirred, not a leaf on a tree, not a rustle from behind the closed hen room door, no sign of life at all in the barn. Even the coyotes' own breathing was soundless.

Then, belly flat to the earth, the larger brother began to crawl toward a gully that dipped low under the goat pasture fence. It was a very narrow passage, barely wide enough to allow for the coyote's well-developed torso to scrape through without touching the wire his father had taught them from experience to dread. Once safely under, he stood up and stared at his brother.

Casting fearful looks back over his shoulder, the smaller coyote followed his brother. When he came to the fence he stopped, cowering at the memory of the fire it held. Then he, too, dropped to his belly and slowly, slowly inched through the gully. He stood up and looked to his brother who was staring into the black interior of the goats' shed. The starlight was so muted that even the two coyotes, used to night-traveling, could barely discern shapes huddled in sleep.

Inch by inch the coyotes advanced until they stood ten feet from the five sleeping goats. The twins were nestled against Clara, noses tucked under their knees. Vetch lay near her head, Clover in the arch of her haunch.

The bold coyote turned his head to flash instructions to his brother, then went into his crouch to spring. The other tensed to follow him.

At the far end of the shed Hiram shifted his weight and Clara, hearing him, lifted her head. Instantly the lead coyote sprang for Clover. Clara screamed. Blitzen woke and lunged for the smaller intruder, catching him across the shoulder with his right horn just as he turned toward Vetch.

Clover gave one terrified and piteous cry as the first coyote slashed her throat. He bared his fangs to finish the job, but out of the chaotic dark something flattened him. Like a fearful demon Clara struck, butting him again and again and trampling him with her sharp cloven hooves. The coyote shrieked.

His frightened brother dropped Vetch and ran as the barn exploded in bedlam. Hens squawked, goats bleated, horses thundered into the barnyard, snorting and squealing. Returning to her mangled baby, Clara rent the night with her frantic wails. Up in the house lights went on one after the other. And suddenly, above the din, a scream of pain rose from the gully. The once-bold young coyote, running for his life, had been scorched by the wire of fire.

Finn thought he heard himself scream when his left leg broke his fall out of the Cessna. The foot turned under him, the ankle bone snapped, but his body slid to a stop against a boulder, knocking the wind out of him. When he came to, he heard the crackling sounds of fire from the plane above him. Flames began to engulf the fuselage, smoke poured out of the cockpit, and through it all someone called his name.

"Finn . . ." His father's voice, thin and barely recognizable.

Finn struggled to all fours, gasping for the breath that had been knocked out of him. From his throat he heard the grunting noise pigs make at feed.

"Finn . . ." The voice sounded like that of a ghost.

Clutching at sage grass, pulling himself upward inch by inch, with the broken leg dragging behind, he struggled toward the sound of his father's voice. Smoke filled his eyes and his nose, making him cough and gag.

"I'm coming," he tried to yell, but he couldn't, he couldn't . . . he could not crawl faster up the precipitous slope. His breath whistled and whined, but the only sound from the Cessna was that of crackling fire. Summoning the last of his power, Finn lunged onward until at last he rose to his knees an arm's length from the open door. From it hung his father's blackened hand.

Instinctively Finn reached for it, but the heat was fiercer than anything he could imagine, and he turned away, covering his face. Behind him there was a muted explosion and a sucking noise as the fuel tank caught fire. A light brighter than sunlight blinded him.

Finn sat bolt upright. An odd sound filled his room—grunts, like pigs at feed. He held his breath and it stopped. His grandmother stood in the door, her hand still on the light switch.

"Get up, Finny," she said. "Something got Clover."

Finn was shaken by the sight of Clover's torn body. She lay crumpled and gasping in the straw of the goat shed, her head askew and her throat gaping. In the beam from Gram's flashlight the blood looked black. He thought he was going to throw up, but he forced the bile down.

"I need you to help me settle everyone down while we wait for Doc Roberts," Gram had told him on the way to the barn. By swinging his crutch wide and taking giant steps with his good leg, Finn was just able to keep up with her.

"I can't get the horses to come in from the pasture so I can close the barnyard gate, and poor Clara is frantic. He must have tried for Vetch first and got scared off, because she's bleeding, too. She's going to be okay, but Clover . . ." She gave Finn's shoulder a little shove. "Here, take this blanket and roll her in it while I go for the horses. I don't want any of them out tonight. If it's coyotes they won't be back, but if it's that other one—he may just try again."

As Finn watched, Clover turned her head and regarded him through dazed, unseeing eyes. He forced himself to pick up the wounded kid and lay her on the horse blanket Gram had given him; then he rolled it up and cradled her in his lap until Dr. Roberts arrived. To his surprise, his grandmother turned pale when the vet asked her to hold Clover while he sewed her up. Also to his surprise, Finn found he was able to watch unblinking as Doc sedated the kid and stitched the gaping wound closed. By the time Finn tumbled back onto his mattress it was three o'clock in the morning.

"Your grandmother's sure it was the one they call a coydog," Julia blurted when she saw Clover the next day.

The one thing that unfailingly rattled Julia was the suffering of any animal. Finn put his good hand on her shoulder and squeezed it.

"She keeps saying a coyote wouldn't just kill for the sake of killing, the way a dog would. But, Finn, I bet whatever almost killed Clover was going to eat her, and something scared him off."

Finn frowned. It troubled him that his grandmother had made up her mind about the culprit. For some reason that he didn't understand, he was convinced that the near slaughter was the work of a coyote—maybe two coyotes. *"Why not?"* he wanted to ask. *"Don't they hunt in packs?"* And before he could put up his guard, an image flew into his mind:

His broken body crouched on the treeless Wyoming mountainside on the second night after the crash, shivering with cold and exhaustion and a fear that had become like an extra limb; four yellow-eyed gray coyotes sitting twenty feet away in a semi-circle around him.

Quickly he banished them.

As though answering his question, Julia said more calmly, "They say coyote parents teach their young to kill their prey one by one. I don't see how they can be sure . . . Well, anyway, what does it matter? At least Clover's not dead."

But it does matter, Finn said to himself. *I don't know why, but it really does matter to me.*

Toq knew that the coyote pups had nearly killed one kid and wounded the other. The thought of taking one for himself had continued to cross his mind, but something about the farm scene stirred a memory— the lights of the house at night or the sight of the tall boy crossing the lawn or the grazing habits of the horses—Toq didn't know what it was, but it turned him away from taking a kid. Instead, he roamed the countryside killing what wildlife he could find to survive.

One night, as he was crossing the high pasture on his way back to his den, he heard sounds in the pinewood. Toq sat down on his haunches in the deeper shadow of the maple to wait. He had learned that a man would soon emerge from the wood, cut diagonally across the pasture to his right, and climb into his truck hidden in the woods beyond. Tonight, Toq could smell, he had the dog with him.

To his surprise the man did not come out of the wood. He stayed and stayed. Toq was tired. His only kill had been two field mice. He had filled his belly with water from a brook on the way home and even that had not slaked his hunger, because the water ran low and was full of silt. He decided to enter the pinewood from another direction, lower down and farther to the west; then he could cut uphill north and eastward to his den, thereby making sure the dog would not catch his scent.

Hugging the old fence line around the pasture, he stole downhill and made his way to the edge of the wood farthest from where the man usually entered. Although Toq had lived in the wood for nearly four years, this was new territory for him, so used was he to following certain trails of his own making. In order to find his way without making a sound, he had to crouch low and move very slowly through the mesh of dead twigs. When he heard the man still moving around near the abandoned well farther to the east, he paused and decided to shift his direction once again.

A sudden noise startled him. He froze, straining to make out what it was. Then, out of a past he had never really known, he recognized the sound of a dog tag jingling. The man whistled and Toq heard the dog turn in the wood and head back toward his master. But the sound, nearer than he expected, rattled Toq. Hastily he changed direction once again; blindly he stumbled into an even denser thicket. And as he did so the steel jaws of a forgotten trap, set twenty years before, closed over his right foreleg and pinned him fast.

"I don't understand what the hell is going on," Jack said to Pinky when they met the next day. He handed him some bindles of cocaine. "Ever since we've used this drop somebody's fiddling with the stuff. Never the money, just the dope. That kid I sold to from the last batch is sick as a dog. You never told me it would be like this, Pinky. I'm scared of Rafe and I want out."

"You ain't getting out of anything, kid," Pinky told him. "You're in for the duration."

"But, Pinky, listen—something's wrong. Somebody is on to us . . . You know Rafe: He finds out somebody's been takin' a chunk and cutting it, he'll—well, he'll fix him good," he added lamely. "I'm scared."

"Shut up, Jack," Pinky snapped. "Just shut up. Go on home, now—I got work to do."

Vetch's wound was superficial and Clover's healed slowly but well. The barnyard resumed its peaceful ways. The last week of July passed, still with no sign of rain.

One day Julia said to Finn, "Remember that fort we built years and years and years ago, when we were little? Let's make a picnic supper and go see if we can find it again. Then, when it's dark, we can go on up to the top of the old pasture above the wood and watch the full moon rise."

She turned to Finn's grandmother. "Remember the time we did that? It was the last year you had the herd—I remember a whole bunch of us sat up there when it was still real pasture and we sang songs until the moon came up. Want to do that tonight, Finn?"

Finn smiled, glad to have any plan to fill the dreaded evening hours. The smile felt good; it was nice not to have his cheek pulled tight by stitches anymore.

Gram packed them a picnic which Finn carried on his back along with a thermos of cold water. His cast had been replaced by a lighter one the week before, and he had switched from a crutch to a cane, but the expedition into the pinewood would be a challenge, he knew—much farther than he had ventured on foot since leaving the Cody hospital. Julia carried a tarpaulin and a long-sleeved shirt in her backpack—"Just in case it's chilly later," she said hopefully—and they set forth at five o'clock.

When they opened the gate at the end of the long horse pasture and came face-to-face with the wall of pines, Julia asked, puzzled, "Didn't we go in from somewhere along here? But there's nothing, not even a hole anymore."

They stood at the southeast corner of the pinewood. So solid was its phalanx of boughs that Finn felt as discouraged as Julia sounded. Idly he stumped to the right a few paces, searching for any sign of the path they had labored over so long ago. Something about the way a white rock protruded from the dry earth at the edge of the wood triggered a memory: Here, wasn't it here they had started? Wasn't that rock their entrance post?

With his good hand Finn pushed aside a bough and peered into the darkness. Yes. Very faintly, but unmistakably, a path wound its way through the web. Without sunlight nothing had grown to replace all the twigs and branches they had cut. He waved to Julia.

"It's not even any cooler in here out of the sun," Julia puffed as they made their way slowly up the slope, slithering on the slippery bed of needles. "I wish we'd cut a *taller* path while we were at it. Lordy, we must have been midgets back then."

Back then it had seemed to take forever to reach the fort, but now they came upon it far sooner than Julia's childhood image remembered. Right away they saw the new path.

"Who do you suppose made that?" Julia asked. "Look, Finn, it seems to go straight up toward the pasture. And here—see?—the ground's sort of scuffed up. Do you suppose it's animals?"

Finn bent down and picked a cigarette stub off the pine needles.

"Oh my gosh, not animals. Kids sneaking a smoke, the way we used to. It doesn't feel the way it did when we were little, though, does it?" she added wistfully.

They turned to the well. By leaning over the wall Finn and Julia could easily see, eight or ten feet below, the rocks and rubble that covered the bottom.

"Imagine us climbing up and down that ladder . . ."

They settled themselves on the stone rim. Julia took off her pack and Finn unhitched the water bottle from his belt and offered it to her.

"Why do you suppose we ever played in this gloomy old wood, anyway?" she asked. As usual she went on as though Finn were going to answer. "I think it was Penny's idea. I think it was the summer we used to play Capture the Flag with the Thompson kids and one week it rained and rained and we couldn't play outside and the three of us drove the grown-ups berserk playing in the house and finally one day Penny said, 'Let's go up to the pinewood and find Gram's old springhouse. We won't get wet in those woods if it starts to rain again and we can make a fort and Finn can be the Indian—'"

Julia handed the thermos back and fell silent, overcome at having remembered Finn's sister so clearly that her own voice had sounded like Penny's.

"Oh, Finn," she said softly. "I know you mind

awfully, but I do wish you'd talk to me about her. It's not fair, you never speaking . . ."

Finn sat without moving as all his soldiers took up their arms. *Please. Please. Please stop. Get away from my fort. I don't want to hurt you.*

"I miss her, too—you know that . . . We could help each other out—"

"I can't," he wanted to say. *"Don't you see I can't? I can't and I won't—please stop."*

The air in the wood was oppressive; no sunlight reached the bed of needles, and nothing stirred. Then, off to the west and below them, a low whine broke the silence. Finn and Julia looked at each other.

"Did you hear that?" she asked.

Finn got up, straining with his whole body to hear the faint noise again. Nothing. Seconds passed. Finn had started to sit down when it came again: an animal noise, more like a groan than a whine, and a barely audible clink, as though a chain had been pulled.

Julia leaped to her feet. "What is it, Finn? Do you think we should—"

But Finn was already on his knees and one hand, headed for the sound, with Julia on all fours behind him. Off the path they had to force their way through the dry blackened limbs, stopping every few feet to listen. Each time the silence seemed to go on forever, until they heard the low sound again and were able to point their course toward it.

A full half hour passed before they found him. When they did, Toq bared his teeth and dared them to approach. Four days in the trap had left him almost mad with pain and thirst and fear. He was visibly thinner, his coat had come out in patches, and the foreleg held in the trap was shredded from his efforts to chew himself free.

Finn could hardly believe his eyes. No doubt about it, this was the animal he had first seen all those years ago, then again last week. He would have known him anywhere. The image of the coyotes on the Absaroka mountainside returned to him. For two nights and one whole day they had watched him. By the time he was rescued, he had come to fear being left entirely alone even more than knowing that the coyotes waited for him to die. But this animal was no coyote. This animal was altogether different. The moment Finn saw him in the trap he felt no fear at all. He squatted awkwardly on the bed of needles and studied the trapped animal.

In desperation Toq drew back on his haunches, but his deep hazel eyes—dulled now by pain—never left Finn's face.

"Oh, oh, oh, the poor thing—it's him," Julia breathed. "How're we ever going to get him free?"

Finn again unfastened the thermos from his belt. He filled the cup to the brim, then very slowly inched closer to the trap and set the cup down before retreating cautiously back to Julia. All the while Toq watched Finn's face. When his eyes turned to the cup of water, he gave a little groan and trembled.

"It's okay, boy, drink it," Julia said in a soft singsong voice. "It's okay, we won't hurt you." And then in a whisper to Finn, "How *can* we help him? He's so fierce."

Finn nodded toward the trap. Toq was up on three legs. He hobbled the short distance to the cup, dragging the chain behind him. Before drinking he glared at Finn in warning. Then he lapped the small cup dry. When Finn moved forward to refill it, Toq growled but did not bare his teeth. After two more cups, the thermos was empty.

"Now what?" Julia asked. "If we go for help, they'll want to shoot him because of Clover and those lambs over at the Thompsons' farm. Oh, Finn, I just know he didn't attack Clover. He looks too—too—too noble, you know what I mean? I almost feel we could ask him. Oh, what's the use. Your grandmother thinks he did it. *She* won't want him loose."

While she talked, Finn was forming a plan. He pulled his T-shirt over his head, undid his belt buckle, and pulled the belt out of the loops of his jeans. Julia watched him.

"Oh," she said. "I get it. You're going to try to muzzle him with that shirt and belt his jaws shut?"

Finn edged a little closer to the trap. His ankle was throbbing painfully and he moved very slowly, but he was not afraid.

Julia said, "I'll go back to the fort and get the picnic. Don't do anything till I get back. Please, Finn, promise you won't try—"

Finn waved her away. He snapped off the lower twigs of a pine and propped himself against the trunk.

The wolf-dog and he regarded each other. The water had allowed saliva to form in Toq's mouth and when he panted drool now ran off his tongue. Finn looked at the foreleg. It was a mess. He could see white bone under the savaged flesh. The steel teeth of the trap met on either side of the leg above the paw.

Once before, when he and his dad were hiking in Wyoming, they had come across a house cat in a trap not unlike this one. He remembered that his father was able to pull the jaws apart without too much difficulty. The cat had scratched him viciously for his efforts. Finn remembered how they both had laughed. Now his eyes filled with tears and as usual he clenched his jaw and brushed them away. Looking up again, his eyes met Toq's and he felt that the trapped animal understood.

Julia returned with the food from their picnic bag. She unwrapped a sandwich and the hybrid's ears pricked forward. Julia started toward him on her knees, but Finn laid his hand on her outstretched arm and took the sandwich from her. When he edged toward the trap, Toq backed off. He laid his ears back and lifted one side of his lip, but he did not snarl. Instead, he gave a little cry as the movement caused the steel teeth to tear at the wounded leg.

It took until nightfall, but Finn and Julia set the hybrid free. In the end they didn't need to use the belt. Finn stuffed the rolled-up T-shirt in Toq's mouth and Julia wrapped her strong arms around his neck from behind. Toq struggled briefly and then held still while Finn strained to wrench apart the stiff jaws of the old trap. They opened hard and Finn wished he could yell out the pain to his hand, but finally the mangled leg slipped loose. Instantly, before Finn could examine the damage, Toq struggled out of Julia's grasp and was gone from their sight, melting away on three legs into the dark wood.

Finding their way back to the fort was a problem. The sun was down and the full moon had only just begun to rise; neither shed light into the dense growth. Twice they turned the wrong way before coming upon the well almost by accident. Finn slipped on the empty picnic bag, and Julia quickly filled it with the untouched soda bottles meant for their supper.

"I don't like this wood anymore. Let's go home. Now," she said. "Let's come back another time to watch the moon."

And, snapping off twigs along the way, they followed their childhood path cautiously to the moonlit horse pasture. It wasn't until they got to the kitchen door that Julia remembered she'd left her backpack at the well.

Chapter 4

LATE IN THE AFTERNOON, A FEW DAYS LATER, Julia and Finn brought a basket of vegetables into the kitchen and laid it on the table.

"The weather's so much nicer today, Finn and I are going to try for that moonrise again while you're at the school board meeting," Julia told Finn's grandmother. "It'll be my last chance—for this month, anyway." Julia was leaving for her dance camp the next day.

"Good idea. It should be almost cool tonight, for a change, and the moon's still very full."

"I left my backpack up at the fort and I need it for camp, so we'll pick it up on our way through the pinewood." She looked quickly at Finn, as though to ask, *Shall we tell her about the hybrid?* But he shook his head, so Julia hurried on. "By the way—did we tell you, there's a new path up there? It goes straight up to the pasture. Looks like some kids have been smoking in the woods. They must have made the path."

Finn's grandmother frowned. "I know; you told me. But I forgot to worry about it. It's bad enough they're smoking at all, but in this dry weather and in that dry wood . . . by the way, Julia, dear, it looks *as though* kids have been smoking, not *like*."

Finn actually laughed silently, partly with relief because Julia hadn't slipped about the wolf-dog, but also because his grandmother had been after him and Penny all their lives about grammar. She had very particular rules.

It was well after eight o'clock before they started for the heifer pasture, hoping to have enough daylight to find their way through the pinewood and catch the moon just as it broke over the horizon sometime after nine.

"I wish we'd see him," Julia said on the way to the fort. "I bet he has a den somewhere in these woods, but you know darn well he'll stay clear of us. I just worry and worry about how he's ever going to feed himself with that bad leg. Maybe you'll get to see him while I'm away."

Because the trees were packed so close and the slope tilted east, the light was even dimmer at dusk than they'd expected. It was too dark to see anything on the wall around the well, but even running their hands along the top failed to turn up the backpack.

"Lucky you brought a flashlight. I could have sworn I left it right here," Julia said. "Do you suppose those kids swiped it the next time they came to smoke? Amazing to think of anyone finding this fort . . ."

She kicked the pine needles all around the well and poked among the thickets of twigs encircling the little clearing. As a last resort, she pointed the flashlight toward the bottom of the well.

"Oh, look, Finn, there's my backpack—I must've knocked it over the edge when we picked up the picnic stuff. "

By craning their necks, they could just see the shape of the pack ten feet below, already half covered with needles. A buckle gleamed faintly in the beam. Julia threw one leg over the wall as though to fetch her pack, but Finn grabbed her arm, and she laughed.

"Oh, right," she said. "No way I could climb out— you'd have to go all the way back to the house and find our old ladder."

She swung her leg back and stood up. "Oh, well, it doesn't matter, if you'll lend me yours for camp. My mom will probably kill me, but we can come get it another time."

The ring of black trunks and branches began to turn to pewter.

"The moon," Julia said. "It's coming— Oh, Finn, come on, let's go *quick* up to the pasture."

She turned and started up the new path. Finn's leg had begun to throb badly. *I should have brought my cane after all,* he thought. He snapped off a bough, stripped it of twigs, and, using that to ease his weight, stumped after her.

— ◆ —

Pinky was beside himself. He had just crested the top of the ridge and was starting across the pasture when he saw two figures emerge from the pinewood at the entrance to the secret path. A girl and a boy. As soon as the boy moved out of the deep shadow of the wood, Pinky realized he must be the one who had survived the plane crash. He moved wrong. He used something that looked like a branch for a cane and the lower half of his left leg was in a cast that shone white in the light of the rising moon. The girl was small and skinny and looked as though she could move fast. Pinky stepped back into the moon-cast shadow of the tree line above the pasture and watched the pair. His mind, disheveled with longing for cocaine, worked erratically.

What the hell are you doing here? was his first thought.

Then: *Whatever it is, just keep moving. Go on, hurry* up! *Don't you fools* know *this is Rafe's night on?*

His last high was nearly over, and he wanted to shoot the boy for moving so slowly. *I need to get into that wood*—he looked at his watch in the moonlight—*by ten. In and out.*

And finally it dawned on him: *God! Oh, my God— they must've seen the drop!*

He squatted down on his haunches and started to shiver. *To hell with that,* he thought, *I'll find us another drop. They couldn'a found the dope. All that matters now is to get to that delivery before Rafe gets here.* He glanced again at his watch: 9:18.

What the hell *are they doing now?*

Pinky groaned inwardly: The two had reached the maple in the middle of the pasture and stood gazing out over the valley as the fat white July moon cleared the hills and turned the valley silver.

Furiously Pinky watched them watch the moon.

All right, all right, it's up, now you can go away. What the—? Oh, my God—they're sitting down. Jeez-US, they're talking. No. She's talking. What about, for God's sake? He isn't saying a word, so what the hell is she talking about in the middle of this God-forsaken field in the middle of the night? Jeez, Louise . . . How the hell am I gonna get in that wood? I gotta get in that wood before Rafe comes.

The minutes ticked by . . . As the moon rose higher and higher, the shadows where Pinky crouched deepened, and he had to strain his eyes to read his watch.

9:20.

9:23.

9:27.

Rafe was never late. Never. For anything. Were they *ever* going to leave? If they weren't gone in the next twelve minutes, he'd never get at the powder. Never ever.

He felt the shakes coming on at the thought. Maybe he could just get up and walk across the field and— No, that was crazy.

Oh, God save us, they're getting up! His nose twitched. He stood, feeling the beginning of nausea, and watched as the pair looked out over the valley once more.

Then the girl turned to start back toward the pinewood. The boy put out his hand and stopped her. Slowly he put his hands on either side of her face; slowly he leaned down and kissed her lips. For a moment she laid her forehead against his chest while he held her in his arms. Then, leaving the bough behind him, he put his good hand on her shoulder and limped with her to the wall.

Pinky tripped and nearly fell three times in his haste to reach the drop. He knew the path well enough by now to find his way without his flashlight, but the moment he got to the well he turned the beam on the stone wall. Kneeling, he fingered his way around the stones until he found the right place. He removed a small flat stone, reached his hand into a crevice, and drew out the leather pouch. Quickly, his fingers trembling, he untied the thong at the neck of the pouch and tipped several plastic-wrapped packets into his hand.

A crackling noise made him freeze. Terrified, he held his breath. The crackling noise became the sound of footsteps on the path.

Rafe.

No time to hide. Desperation made Pinky crafty. He slipped two packets into his pocket and rose to his feet to greet Rafe when he entered the clearing.

"*Pinky!*—What the—" The voice was harsh with suspicion.

"I've found out who's been messing with our

goods," Pinky blurted. He wished his own voice didn't sound so shaky.

Rafe stared at the packets on the ground in front of Pinky.

"What the—" he said again and took a step toward Pinky.

"Rafe, listen to me." Pinky spoke rapidly. "I was just cruisin' by the farm down there and I saw two kids go into the woods. A girl and a boy with a cast on his foot, the one that fell outta that plane. They went in by the path I found. I don't know how the hell they found it, but I drove all the way around to where we leave the trucks and watched them come out into the field up there—"

Pinky saw the gleam of disbelief glinting in the narrowed eyes. Rafe's fists were curled tight at his sides. He opened one and slipped it into his pocket where something bulged.

Pinky started to shake. Still holding the flashlight, he put his hands on his hips to steady them and then wished he'd wiped his nose first. God, he had to get this over with fast or he'd be dead, either at Rafe's hands or from needing that coke. He didn't know which was worse.

"I watched them snort, up there, under the maple," he said. Inspiration struck. "You can even see the branch the boy used kinda like a crutch—it's still up there. When they left I come right straight to the well to check. They was smart; they put most of it back, but look—" Pinky nodded toward the pile of packets at their feet. "Two bags missing. Just two, but jeez, Rafe, what're we gonna do now?"

Rafe continued to glare at him without moving a muscle. Then he took his hand from his pocket and held it out.

"Give me the light," he said.

He shone the beam on the carpet of needles around the well and saw that someone or something had scuffled them thoroughly.

No hooves or claws, no sign at all of animals, he said to himself. *More like feet with shoes. And there's that old gap in the trees where Pinky came through . . . They could have come in that way.*

He raised the flashlight and scanned the wall of dead limbs. The beam came to rest on the stub of a freshly broken branch. *Could be he's telling the truth,* Rafe thought. *I'll sure as hell find out if he's not.* He turned to face Pinky.

"Pick up the stuff," he said. He held out the pouch. "Put it back."

Pinky hoped Rafe would think it was fear of the trouble they were in that made his fingers tremble. Rafe tucked the bag under his elbow. He bent down, pushed a wad of bills into the drop, and closed it with the stone.

"You touch that and you're dead," he said. "Go back to your truck. Drive straight to my place. I'll meet you there in half an hour."

Stalling, Pinky reached for the zipper of his jeans. "I'll be right with you," he said. "Gotta pee."

Rafe turned on his heel and strode up the narrow path, the beam of light never wavering as it blinked through the trees. Left behind in the dark, Pinky zipped himself up and fumbled in his pocket for a packet. By the time he had extracted one bindle of cocaine and snorted the white powder, his whole body was shaking convulsively. He waited until the drug took over; then, full of what he called control, he hurried after Rafe, plotting, plotting, plotting how to turn this night to his advantage. In his haste he was unaware that one of his precious little bags had fallen to the ground.

Julia left the next morning and Finn missed her even more than he feared he would. He spent the rest of the day in the barn because it made her seem nearer. Hour after hour he moped in the cool, dark lower level, until Monica, tired of watching him, came down from her beam and curled up in his arms.

Finn thought about the evening before. For the first time, Julia had talked seriously about her dancing and what it felt like to talk with your whole body. Going to dance camp was a dream come true, she'd told him. As Finn listened, he realized for the first time how much it meant to her, and he felt jealous.

"But," she had said in her direct way, "I'll miss you, Finn."

That made him feel better. So when they stood up he had kissed her. It had seemed a natural way to say good-bye, but it turned out to be more than that.

Again and again he replayed that brief kiss in his mind. Like a video, he stopped and rewound and kissed her again. His heart had felt so light at the touch of her lips and the feel of her slim body in his arms. He couldn't believe how light it had felt—he had thought he would never feel that way again. It reminded him of—what? Not the two other girls he had kissed. They had been fun, exciting even, but different. When he kissed Julia in the moonlit pasture, he felt as though he had come home. Now, reliving the kiss again, with Monica purring away in his lap, he thought surely the next ten days would never come to an end.

After the pandemonium in the barnyard at Riverview Farm died down on the night Clover was nearly slaughtered, the two coyotes had returned to the wood, hungry, defeated, and angry; but for many days they were too frightened to venture forth again. Instead, they scrounged for mice and crickets. Their bellies growled with hunger. Then, by means only animals know, news reached the pinewood that lambs had been weaned at the Sanders's farm.

The Sanders's place lay north of Riverview Farm, on the far side of the ridge above the pinewood. The evening after Julia went to camp, the coyotes heard the wails of the lambs calling for their dams and they headed toward the sound. It took the father no more than three minutes to find a small gap in the Sanders's wire fence and to shepherd the younger ones into the fold. There they made their kill, ate their fill, and took home a portion to the female. As is the custom of coyotes, they left the corpse hidden in a thicket outside the fold.

News of the kill traveled fast, alarm spreading from one farm to the next. Finn's grandmother heard about the slaughtered lamb the next day.

"I tell you, it's that hybrid. I'm sure of it. We haven't had an outbreak of kills like this in years. Jim Hatch says we all better have a shotgun ready."

She swished out her cup fiercely and set it on the drain board with a thump that nearly cracked it.

Finn knew her well enough to understand that she sounded angry because she was as protective of her animals as was Julia. Nonetheless, he resented her suspicion of "his" animal.

MAYBE NOT, he scrawled on the kitchen blackboard. MAYBE COYOTES.

"Oh, Finn, you live in a dream world," Gram said impatiently and left the kitchen.

Very late the following night Pinky started for the boardinghouse where Rafe lived. Halfway there he lost his nerve and went back to his pickup which he'd parked a block away. With one eye on the lighted window of Rafe's room, he leaned against the door of the truck and reviewed what he planned to say to Rafe.

For weeks he had collected specific signs to back up his suspicion of Rafe: what days Rafe was never seen in town, what nights he hung out in one of the local bars—little pieces of evidence to hold up his sleeve if Rafe ever gave him trouble.

Rafe catching him at the drop was trouble. He

knew he'd convinced Rafe that the kids from the farm had stolen the cocaine. By the time they had met later that night, Rafe had decided to keep the well as a drop for one more week to be certain. Whether it was an inside job—Pinky swallowed as he remembered Rafe looking him in the eye—or just the kids or a plot of the feds in town, Rafe wanted to know for sure before they changed drops.

Now Pinky had found another perfect drop, behind a deserted cabin he used when he hunted in the fall. It was beyond the Sanders's place and Pinky had never seen a trace of human activity there in all his years of deer hunting.

That'll get me in good with Rafe again for starters, he thought.

But the next part wasn't so easy. Once again Pinky rehearsed:

"Rafe," he'd say. *"I got an idea you might like. How about I take over for Jack? That way we don't need to slice the dough three ways. That Jack—he ain't worth much. I got time on my hands. I can handle the high school users. They already know me. I—"*

But here Pinky stopped. What did it matter to Rafe whether Pinky got a bigger slice of the profit? Rafe already took half, why would he care whether his two underlings got more or less money? Would Rafe guess right off that it was the cocaine that Pinky wanted more access to?

No. Not possible. Rafe knew that Pinky knew no user could be trusted to be a dealer. No drug trafficker would dare, no matter how big a fool. Rafe had told them that straight off. That's why Pinky had taken care to hide from Rafe any sign of his addiction on the few occasions they met, and that's why Rafe had been able to believe Pinky's story last night. Pinky knew that he had reached the point where it was almost impossible to disguise his addiction—as hay fever or fear of narcs—but for now he was pretty sure Rafe would still think he was motivated by greed. Let him. What did he care, anyway? He had almost enough on Rafe by now to name his own terms.

Still, Pinky was scared of Rafe and dreaded the bawling out Rafe was going to give him for coming to his boardinghouse. He held out his hands again to be sure they were not shaking and looked both ways up and down the empty street. Then, reminding himself once again of all the blackmail material he had collected, he pushed himself away from the side of the pickup, strode resolutely to the boardinghouse door, and opened it.

"Rafe," he whispered into the dark hall. "Rafe, you home?"

When no one answered, Pinky advanced farther into the hall.

"Rafe?" A louder whisper. Still no answer.

Pinky didn't dare call louder, so he started up the stairs, taking care to test each step for creaks along the way. At the top of the stairs he heard a mumbling voice. It was speaking in a foreign tongue so it took Pinky a second to realize it was Rafe's voice. No one else spoke, so Pinky figured Rafe was talking on the telephone. Pinky crept down the hall and stopped outside Rafe's door.

By taking very shallow breaths, he could overhear what Rafe was saying. Rafe didn't sound very expert in whatever the language was, and after a few minutes, Pinky heard him say in English, "Okay, Pedro, you just remember it's your ass, too, if we get caught. You tell your friends in Mexico that, amigo: Your ass as well as mine."

Pinky needed to hear no more. This was better than cutting out Jack. Now he *really* had the goods on Rafe: Rafe was double-crossing them all. Without waiting to hear more, Pinky tiptoed quickly down the stairs, plotting, plotting, plotting.

Julia had left on Friday, the first of August. On Mondays and Tuesdays Finn's grandmother worked at the town library. By the time he finished the list of chores she had left for him on Tuesday, Finn had run out of ideas as to how to keep his mind off what happened in the Absarokas and was almost beside himself with restlessness and boredom. He didn't feel like reading, so once again he laid *The Catcher in the Rye* aside and decided to go get Julia's backpack. It would give him something to do during the long afternoon, and maybe—just maybe—he'd catch sight of the wolf-dog.

He had begun to make a little progress writing left-handed and had taken to leaving notes for Gram on the blackboard in the kitchen when she was working or out. Now, his tongue between his teeth, he wrote, GONE FOR JULIA'S PACK AT SPRINGHOUSE. BACK BY FIVE. With a hint of the old Finn, he added, SHALL DESPATCH ANY SMOKERS I MEET ALONG THE WAY.

He thought about using the cane or even the crutch again, knowing he'd make better time, but realized that time didn't mean a thing. That was the trouble—he had all the time in the world. Instead, he took their old rope ladder out of the attic closet. It was light enough to sling over his shoulder and looked strong enough to hold him still. Anyway, it might be fun to try it out again in the well. Ordinarily, Finn was sure, he could have managed now without a ladder, because of his height and strength; but with one ankle only partly mended and one hand still raw to the touch, he knew he had no choice.

It was his third trip up the path in less than a month. Each time he and Julia had snapped off more twigs and small branches as they passed, so now he hardly needed to bend over. When Finn reached the well, he sat down, hoping that the wolf-dog might appear. An image of the wild animal filled his mind's eye. Again Finn saw him stop halfway across the meadow and the memory of the look they'd exchanged made the hair stand up on his arms. With fierce concentration he visualized the animal—its powerful build and fine large head. He visualized, too, the wounded leg and willed that it heal. Then he tried whistling softly. But Toq did not appear.

After a while Finn turned his attention to the task of retrieving Julia's backpack. He hooked the ladder over the wall and climbed down into the well. The rocky bottom was far rougher than he remembered. He nearly stumbled when he bent to pick Julia's pack out of its bed of needles. When he set his foot on the first rung of rope and looked up the stone shaft to the top, Finn felt a little shudder of fear. He never could have made it without a ladder, even without his injuries. What if he hadn't left that note for Gram? Who would ever find him, here in this dungeon in the dark pinewood? Once out of the well, he flopped down on the ground, tired and sore all over. Well, at least Julia had her pack back.

It was then that his eye fell on a small white square of plastic wrap half hidden in the pine needles. The bed of needles was so thick that he could easily have missed it. Curious, he bent forward and picked it up and in that instant, without warning, he was transported out of the present.

Last spring, in tenth grade, for the first and only time, he had seen other packets like the one in his hand. One of his friends—a kid named Jerry—had led him to a knot of boys and girls gathered behind the high school. The one who looked as though he was in charge was a stranger to Finn, older than the rest, with a scarred face and a runny nose. Finn remembered the nose particularly; it seemed queer to him that anyone would have to keep wiping his nose on a warm day in May. In his hand was a collection of little packets just like this.

He and Jerry remained on the outskirts of the group, until Jerry turned to Finn and said, "Want to try some?"

And Finn had hesitated. *Why not? Why not, just this once? Jerry had, Jerry would do it again, Jerry said cocaine was fantastic.*

"It'll cost you twenty bucks for one packet."

That was what decided it. Finn didn't have twenty dollars on him. He didn't even have much money back in his fine new bedroom, because he'd just spent all his earnings on a bike. He guessed he could borrow the money from his mom, but . . .

"I'll think about it," he told Jerry. "Maybe next week, after we get back from Memorial Day weekend."

Finn remembered the scene as clearly as though it were happening now. *That was a different world,* he thought, *a different time, a different life . . . In that life Finn went home still thinking about the dealer and his classmates behind the school building. He had been surprised—in fact, shocked—by the number of familiar faces gathered around the scar-faced man. "Good guys" like Jerry as well as troublemakers. Finn had read about what drugs did to you. His parents had talked openly and often with him and Penny about the danger of trying any of them. Yet here was Jerry taking cocaine. He didn't look any different than he ever had in all the years Finn had known him, but then he'd only snorted twice, according to what he told Finn.*

Finn had swung his book bag onto his bed and made a bundle of dirty clothes to wash before they took off tomorrow to visit Uncle Matt. When Penny came into the laundry room with her own pile, he told her about the dealer.

"You know anyone who actually does drugs?" he asked.

Whenever their parents asked them, they both said no, which was mostly the truth. As a family they never really got around to talking about specific cases.

"Sally's brother does, but he's a grade ahead of me."

Car doors slammed outside and Finn said, "Here come Mom and Dad. Let's not talk about it now."

And so the four of them had spent the evening packing and poring over maps and telephoning Uncle Matt and going out to a restaurant for supper. It was Penny's turn and she chose her old favorite, Friendly's. That was nice; Finn had always liked Friendly's, too.

Once unstoppered, the memories poured on and on . . .

They'd even talked Mom into going to the movies, though she said, "But how are we going to get a crack-of-dawn start if we go to the movies?" And then, "Oh, well, okay. Holidays are holidays."

When they got home from the movies, Mom made them all milk shakes and they sat up for an hour deciding what they were going to do on Uncle Matt's ranch. It was a particularly pleasant evening. No one argued about plans, his father was more relaxed than Finn had seen him in months, and his mother got the giggles describing the first time she rode a horse. Finn considered bringing up the incident in the school yard, but as *he was turning the idea over in his mind, his father stood up, yawned, and said: "Bed. Now. It is one o'clock in the morning and we are supposed to be taking off in eight, I repeat eight, hours."*

Even though they all overslept, the next morning was nice, too. Penny allowed herself to be dragged out of bed without howling in protest; their dad stayed cool and only laughed when he saw the kitchen clock; and his mom—Finn's heart swelled—his mom had reached out and hugged him as they left the house to join the other two in the car. "I love you, Finny," she said. Only when they arrived at the little airport to find the weather changing did the mood become serious.

"Come on, son," Finn heard his father's voice say, as clear as though he addressed him right there in the pinewood.

He stared unseeing into the musty darkness, until once again a faint familiar aroma took him by surprise. He sniffed. Pine tar. Concentrating on each breath, he inhaled slowly again and again. Yes. Pine tar. Like the resin his mother used in her paints. The air in the pinewood was so filled with her presence, that Finn was tempted to turn and look at her. But, no. He closed his eyes. He decided to believe she was really there.

What am I to do? he asked her. *Tell me, Mom. I'm stuck. I can't—I won't—it hurts too much to look back, and I can't face moving forward. Can't face mov-*

ing. Don't know how. Even when Julia's here, I just get through each day by the skin of my teeth. What am I going to do when school starts? Gram says some doctor may help me get my voice back, but oh, my God, Mom, what will it say? *Sometimes it feels as though there's this little voice inside, but I don't dare listen to it. If I let it out I'll have lost control and I can't do that—I'd blow away if I did that.* His eyes filled with tears.

This stuff I found up here—it's cocaine. Did you know that, Mom? Looks like the kids around here are trying it. Julia says there are pushers down in town. Did you know Jerry tried it? Says it's fantastic. What do you think, Mom? Things are so different now— would you mind if I tried it, too? Would you understand? Because I don't know what to do, Mom. I don't even know who I am anymore. Maybe this little white pack of powder would help me find my way back, help me forget what happened in the Absarokas, let it go, get on with my life.

Finn stifled a great sob collecting in his chest. His hand closed hard around the plastic packet. Maybe. Maybe this was the answer. Fantastic, Jerry had said. Fantastic . . .

Oh, Mom, I wish you were here, where I could see you. Touch you. I wish I could tell you how much I miss you. I wish you and Dad knew I tried to get you all out. If only you knew . . .

The small white plastic square felt cool on his palm; a dusting of earth still clung to the bottom. He tossed it up and down a couple of times.

How white the powder is. Looks like medicine. Those doctors in Cody, they didn't give me anything to make me feel good . . . Jerry told me how to snort. Maybe . . .

Finn stared at it a little longer, until something splashed on the packet and he realized he was crying, so he slipped it into his pocket and dried his eyes with his sleeve. He took a long slow breath, but he knew his mother had gone.

Were you really here? he wondered sadly.

Toq was lying hidden in a thicket fifteen feet away. He laid his head on his good paw. The other leg was nearly healed but pained him still. Soundless and invisible, the wounded wolf-dog regarded the wounded boy who had saved his life.

Thursday afternoon Finn's grandmother came into the kitchen, set two bags of groceries on the kitchen table, and sighed. "This heat—honestly, I don't remember it ever being so hot for so long. I got your favorite ice cream."

The long, hot, lonely day had driven Finn nearly to distraction. Gram had not left him anywhere near enough to do this endless week. Over and over he had considered the possibility of trying the cocaine. There it lay in his bureau drawer, hidden beneath his underwear and the recorder.

So easy.

No one here.

Fantastic, Jerry had said . . .

Once he had even started for the stairs, but the image of Julia stopped him. With one foot on the bottom step he replayed their kiss, then shook his head and went back to the kitchen.

He had breathed a sigh of relief when he heard his grandmother's car in the lane. Helping her put the food away, he even managed to smile when she mentioned the ice cream. Ice cream, he decided, would help a little.

But suddenly Gram said, "Oh, curses, curses! I must have left it on the counter. Oh, no." She pawed through the remaining groceries. "Yep. That's just what happened. I got to chatting with the checkout girl while she put it in a plastic bag and—" Gram looked up and saw Finn's face fall. "I'll go back. Tell you what, Finny. You come, too, and I'll drop you off at the swimming hole for a quick dip, run into town for the ice cream, and pick you up twenty minutes later."

Finn hesitated. The day had been endless and the heat really was appalling. Maybe . . .

Gram, reading his face, said, "No one will be swimming at this hour, and if anyone's there, we'll just keep going." She smiled. "And *you* can go in to get the ice cream. The Grand Union's positively frigid from air-conditioning."

Why not? thought Finn, and he limped upstairs and changed into his trunks.

"Here—take this towel," Gram said, draping it over his shoulders when she let him out at the river.

"Now, get *cool*," said Gram as she turned the car. "That's an order."

Sitting on the riverbank in his trunks, Finn took off his cast and wrapped it in his towel. Then he slid quickly into the moving water. How cool it felt. Here and there unexpected jets of really cold water teased his nearly naked body, and he rolled onto his back and let the current carry him downstream.

A little farther on he saw the swinging branch and what looked to be the very same old rope hanging from it. Maybe, when Julia came back, maybe some evening, if the river really was always deserted at this hour, they might—

Suddenly he heard a motor on the dirt track that ran down to the river.

Damn, he thought. *Damn, damn, damn.* And he swam under one of the overhanging vines of honeysuckle.

Down to the river's edge came two strangers. One was thin and dark and dressed in clothes that had a cityish look to them. The other was squarely built and muscular with heavy dark brows. They spoke intently to each other as they walked, but Finn could not hear what they were saying until they stopped on the little muddy beach of the swimming hole, not twenty feet from where he lay.

"Now, as to dis Peenky, you dam' sure 'bout him, Rafe?" The slight man spoke with an accent Finn did not recognize. "We don' want no more trouble like last time. Your feds, we can handle, but not fools. My people in Mexico City—dey don' like blood, but dey not gonna stand for no fonny beezness. Dis Peenky—you watch him good."

"I told him to come here before he meets his high school contact at six. Said I had a new pusher for him to meet—*from Boston*, I said. He sure as hell don't know about the Mexican connection. You can see him for yourself, but like I told you, he's in too deep to risk any funny business."

Beneath the trailing vines Finn heard footsteps approach along the path to the river and he drew further under cover. The leaves got in the way, but he could make out the contours of a flabby man who looked to be in his early thirties.

Must be Pinky, Finn thought.

"That your towel back there?" Finn thought Pinky sounded as though he was challenging the one called Rafe.

"Didn't see any towel." Rafe, evidently unused to being taken by surprise, spoke sharply. Then he shrugged. "Must be some kid still swimmin' downriver. This here's Pete—that Boston contact I told you about, Pinky. I got a new list for you for over to Ludlow. Pete here brought it with the latest load of goods."

Pinky wiped his nose. Then he held out his hand, which Finn could see trembled very slightly.

"Okay, so give it to me," he slurred.

To Finn, in his hiding place, the fat man sounded slightly drunk and defiant.

The man from Mexico tautened. He frowned and looked quickly at Rafe.

"It's up at the truck," Rafe said in a cold, even voice. "We'll be right along. I got business to finish with Pete."

Pinky turned and retraced his steps.

The moment he was out of sight, the Mexican whirled on Rafe and said, "You crazy, mon? Dat man's a user. I can spot 'em a mile off. Mon, you can't trust no *user*."

Finn felt a little shudder of fear at the violence of the voice. Instinctively he half closed his eyes as though to shut out the scene. Through his lashes and the veil of leaves the sparkle of the water grew brighter. Then a clicking noise caught his attention and his eyes flew open again in time to see another sparkle: sunlight on the dagger of a switchblade the dark man held in his hand.

"Take it easy, Pedro," said Rafe. "He gets hay fever, that's all. It's haying season here. Put that thing away. I know what I'm doing. I find out he's using"—he glanced at the knife Pedro was refolding—"I'll take care of Pinky. Now let's get outta here in case there's kids around."

He took Pedro's elbow and the two started walking quickly back to the trail and were soon out of earshot. No sooner did Finn hear the car start than he swam the few yards upstream to where he'd left his towel. A minute or two later Gram came to pick him up.

Once they got home, he went to the blackboard

and laboriously spelled out what he had seen. His grandmother shook her head, amazed.

"I guess Julia was right," she said. "I thought she must be exaggerating, about a drug ring and all. But honestly—here, in a small town in *Vermont*? Well, I'm glad we live out here on the farm, that's all I can say. Here, Finny, have some ice cream."

Jack came out of the poolroom in the shabbiest part of town, crossed the railroad tracks, and headed up the unlit narrow street that led to his house. It was past midnight and if his mother was still awake, she was going to give him hell for coming in so late. The thought irritated him at the same time that it made him hasten his pace. Here he was, earning big-time money in a dangerous business, and he had to worry about obeying bedtime rules like a kid. Jeez—

Suddenly, from out of the pitch-dark shadows, a figure stepped in front of him. Jack thought his heart had stopped for good.

"I want to talk to you, kiddo," said Rafe, and he took Jack by the neck of his T-shirt and pulled him into the alley behind an empty store.

"Wh-wh-wh-" For the life of him, Jack could not get out a word.

"Now listen to me, you listen up real good."

At the sound of footsteps on the deserted street, Rafe stopped talking. He put one large hand over Jack's mouth and the other around his scrawny neck. Jack could hardly breathe. The footsteps faded down the street toward the pool hall, and Rafe removed both hands.

Putting his face right up against Jack's, he growled softly, "You listenin'?"

Jack nodded. He couldn't even swallow, much less speak.

"I want to know if Pinky's usin'. And especially I want to know if he's usin' our stuff."

In instant replay, the scene at his truck last month flashed before Jack: *"I don't understand what the hell is going on . . . Somebody's fiddling with the stuff . . . Somebody is on to us . . . You know Rafe . . ."*

And Pinky's answer: *"Shut up, Jack. Go on home now. I got work to do."*

Now, his throat aching from dryness, Jack managed to croak: "No. I dunno. No."

"'No. I dunno. No.'" Rafe's lips drew back, showing small pointed teeth in the near-total darkness of the alley. "What's that mean?"

Jack's mind whirred. "Means I don't know, Rafe," he managed. "Just once I wondered—"

"Yeah? Well, next time you wonder, you pay attention. You wonder good and hard, and then you come to me and we'll wonder together, the two of us. We're goin' to find out about our friend Pinky for sure. And then we're gonna take care of him, you can bet your ass."

Julia's dance camp seemed to Finn to go on forever. By the Sunday night she was due home he had exhausted all the small tasks Gram gave him to do. He had weeded the vegetable garden to perfection, helped his grandmother put up pickles, and even worked a little with Daisy. He found he couldn't sit still enough to read, because the minute he stopped moving he thought about the cocaine. To get his mind off that, he tried twice more to find the hybrid in the pinewood, each time sensing that the animal hovered nearby, but dared not approach. Thank God this week was over.

Tomorrow Julia will come, he said to himself over and over. *Tomorrow, tomorrow.* Julia would persuade Gram that the wolf-dog was innocent. Perhaps she'd stretch the story of their encounter to say he had lost a leg and therefore could not kill something as big as a lamb. *When I wake up tomorrow, she'll be home*, he thought and the relief was like balm to his troubled soul.

He decided to go to bed early so as to make tomorrow come sooner. His grandmother looked up from a sitcom on the television and waved to him as he left the kitchen.

"Good-night, honey," she said. "Sleep well."

But when Finn went up to his room, he stopped thinking about the hybrid or even Julia. Once again, as it had every night since he found it, his mind fastened, with a rapacity that startled him, on the cocaine in his top drawer. Once again he picked it up.

This may be my last chance, he thought, turning the packet over and over in his hand.

Yet once again he laid it back in the drawer and picked up the recorder.

I'll wait for Julia, he decided. *Maybe she'll want to try it with me . . . Maybe. . . Probably not . . . probably she'll say we have to tell Gram . . . That'll put an end to it . . . Put an end to the hybrid, too, I guess . . . if the police go through the pinewood looking for those kids' hangout . . . whatever . . . I'll just wait one more night and see what Julia says.*

In order to stay away from his bureau he went to the window. Standing like a stork on one leg, his forehead pressed agaist the top of the frame, Finn stared sightlessly down at the barnyard. Clouds covered the night sky, promising rain that did not fall. A sudden rustle caught his attention. Unable to identify the sound, he narrowed his eyes and tried to focus on where it came from.

Nothing. Then another little noise, as of a rubbing of one thing against another. Where? The barnyard? Finn could not be sure where and what the noise was over the faint sound of the television downstairs.

What kind of noise do coyotes make when they hunt? he wondered. The coyotes in the Absarokas never seemed to move at all; they simply sat, tongues lolling, and watched him day in and day out.

Finn stayed by the window without moving for several minutes, straining to hear action of any kind in the barnyard. He considered going down there but, still annoyed with his grandmother for suspecting the hybrid, decided he didn't want to have to explain where he was going. Deep down, he had to admit that he didn't want to risk the slightest chance that it really might turn out to be the wolf-dog stalking the goats. After a while he decided without much conviction that he had imagined hearing a noise. He turned away from the window and had just started to undress for the long night ahead, when the sound reached him again.

Carefully, moving it so slowly that even he could not hear it, Finn raised the screen of his window and poked his head out. It was amazing how much better he could see without the wire mesh. A long rectangle of light from the kitchen window fell across the lawn below. Down in the barnyard nothing stirred as far as he could see, although with no starlight, he could not see much.

Finn withdrew his head and raised his hands to lower the screen. Once again, unmistakably this time, he heard what he now recognized without doubt to be branches being pushed aside. He even knew where and what the branches were, though he found it difficult to believe his ears. It was the lilac bush next to the kitchen window. He knew that sound well from windy days when the branches scraped against the old bricks and tapped the windowpanes.

Again he leaned out the window. As he did so, a figure directly below him materialized out of the shadow of the house. It seemed to be a man, though from this perspective Finn could get no clear impression, other than furtiveness and haste. A lilac branch caught the man's sleeve; he turned, muttering, to release it and Finn caught a glimpse of a sullen face and reddish hair. Where had he seen that face before? Something about it was familiar, something had triggered an immediate shudder of fear when he glimpsed it. Just as the man looked up, Finn drew his head in the window. Crouched on the floor, he heard the stranger scuttle away from the house across the lawn. Halfway down the lane an engine started and was gunned, and a vehicle drove past the barn and out onto the road.

Finn hopped and stumbled down the stairs and swung into the kitchen. Startled, his grandmother looked up from the television.

"Hello, what's up?" she asked.

Finn went to the blackboard and wrote: THERE WAS A MAN OUTSIDE WATCHING. He pointed to the kitchen window. His grandmother stood up, frowning. Crossing the linoleum floor in three strides, she flung open the door and squinted into the dark night.

"Which way did he go?" she asked. Finn could tell by the sound of her voice that she was frightened. He was, too. Nothing like this had ever happened on Riverview Farm.

"But why? Why on earth spy on us?" Gram asked. "It just doesn't make any sense. You might think we were part of some kind of gang."

Finn's heart skipped a beat. His face went cold with shock as he remembered the face of the man he had seen at the river. *The cocaine! My God, of course—the cocaine! The man must have been after the cocaine in my room,* Finn thought guiltily. He was the one who had left it at the well! He was probably in trouble for losing some of the goods. Should he write all that out for his grandmother? It all still seemed so unlikely—a bunch of amateur locals involved in big-time drugs. Finn felt another stab of guilt at the thought of telling her about the packet in his drawer. How could he ever *write* the complicated sequence of events that brought it there? No.

He watched his grandmother continue to fuss and fume as she put away some dishes, turned off the TV, put out milk for Monica, and wiped the kitchen counter. By the time she was ready to turn out the light, her voice was normal.

"Well, Finny," she said. "You never know what'll happen these days. Even in Vermont. I'm certainly not going to call the sheriff about one Peeping Tom. Likely as not it's some kid seeing if we have anything to nab. Come on, there's nothing more we can do. Let's go on up. Tonight I'll even lock the door, if I can find the key."

But Finn could not stop thinking about the drug in his bureau and the man at the window. A gang. A drug ring. Not kids. Big time. Thoroughly shaken, he followed his grandmother up the stairs. Once in his room, he didn't even open his bureau drawer, but stripped, turned out the light, and went straight to bed.

Oh, please, let me sleep, he prayed. *Let me sleep until tomorrow when Julia comes home.*

— ❖ —

The fire was the worst. Of the whole three-day nightmare, the fire was the worst of it all. Worse than the terrible drop out of the sky; worse than crashing against the mountainside; worse than falling out of the plane; worse, even, than the two endless, icy nights alone with the four coyotes.

After the fuel tank ignited, flames enveloped the fuselage with a muted sucking roar. Over and behind and through the roar Finn thought he heard his mother cry out. He could not hear what she cried or even if she cried, or maybe it was Penny, or maybe it was the noise the fire made as a draft blew it higher and faster. Everything was happening so fast, Finn felt as though he were caught in one great spinning whirlwind of flame and heat.

The high moaning sound came again and he thrust himself forward and up into the tilted plane and reached through flames to his father, but his father had become a blackened lifeless mass. His father was no longer there, just what was left of his body, and when Finn tried to lunge past the front seat toward where his mother and his sister were, flames enveloped him and he fell back, terrified. As he did so, he knocked against his father's black hand and the fingers seemed to stretch in supplication. For an instant he stared at the hand, then little, pale tongues of fire licked him all over. A piece of the wheel was caught on his left sleeve and burned brightly. Wild with fright he dropped out of the plane and rolled onto his flaming arm. Over and over he rolled, picking up speed as the

105

slope steepened, until at last he plummeted to a stop against a boulder and lost all consciousness.

Hours later he drifted back into his body and opened his eyes. A moonless night had fallen, but above him bright embers cast a pale halo in the sky. Finn had no idea where he was. His hand raged with pain. His ankle throbbed mercilessly. Dry blood tightened the skin of his face. The smell of smoke permeated his whole body; it filled his lungs and made him gag.

Out of the darkness on the other side of the fire he heard a coyote howl: Yip-yip-yip-yowwl. And from somewhere on the other side of the boulder his body was draped across came an answering call: Yip-yip-yip-yoowwl.

With a last spurt of energy the flames of the fallen plane crackled and rose up in a brief blaze of light and went out. Total darkness fell over the Absaroka Range.

While sleep finally overtook Finn and his grand-mother, anxiety ruled the barnyard. The headlights of Pinky's pickup flashed on Daisy's face when he raced down the lane, startling her and sending her in a panic out into the pasture. The two oldest hens stirred and clucked crossly, which woke Clara, who—remember-ing the coyotes—bleated with fright for her twins.

Belle followed her filly out into the dark pasture: When the old mare could not immediately find her, she whickered softly to Hiram and Horace. The two draft horses came awake and lumbered slowly out of the shed. At the farthest end of the pasture, near the gate to the pinewood, the three horses found Daisy, who had forgotten what frightened her and was chomping the dewy night grass. For a while all four horses grazed, until the sound of something moving in the pinewood frightened them again. They moved uneasily back to the shed and stood with heads lowered, until once again sleep fell over the whole barn.

After fleeing Riverview Farm in his pickup, Pinky pulled off the road just below the horse pasture and made his way between the fence and the pinewood to the entrance of the lower trail. There he crouched down to see if any police cars would come to the farm. When time passed and none did, he began to assess the damage done by the cripple seeing him under the window. He was sure that was who it had been. He had been crazy to go there. Crazy. Only a recent hit and his need for more cocaine had given him the courage to do what had seemed a good idea. But it had turned into a near disaster.

Getting all that evidence against Rafe had made him cocky. He had thought nothing would ever make him fear Rafe again. He was wrong. Getting caught stoned tonight would have given Rafe the chance to ditch him once and for all, and no one in the drug world would believe his incriminating evidence against Rafe, because they'd know that he, Pinky, was a junkie and that junkies would say anything for a hit.

And it was true, Pinky admitted to himself in a rare moment of honesty. Like any addict obsessed by need,

Pinky spent most of his waking hours figuring where and when and how he would obtain his next fix. When he discovered that he had lost one-half of the dope he had stolen from last Thursday's drop, Pinky had cursed long and hard. As soon as possible he had made his way back to the well. But although he searched with the thoroughness of desperation, he found no packet, and it didn't take him long, by a process of elimination, to figure out it must have been the two kids after all, or at least the boy. From what he'd seen of the girl, that one time at the Grand Union, Pinky couldn't see her being into cocaine.

He sneered to himself, *So I was right after all, when I told Rafe them kids swiped the stuff. Whaddya know.* And then, like a fool, driven by rage at the tall lame kid, he had nearly blown his advantage sky high . . . Had the kid seen him well enough to recognize him if they ran into each other downtown? When school started in a few weeks, the kid'd be in the same class as Jack. What if Finn saw him and Jack together—would he put two and two together? Once started, one question after another flew into Pinky's mind until every shred of confidence seeped out of his flabby body and into his bed of pine needles.

Why had he gone to Riverview Farm? How did he ever think he could retrieve the lost cocaine? Pinky groaned, but even as he raged at himself for taking such a useless risk, the thought hit him again that a whole packet of bindles—at least ten trips—had been snatched from him and, by God, he would have them back. They were his, by right! Now that he'd seen the layout of the house, he'd go back before that no-good cripple snorted or unloaded the lot. In fact, maybe it was a good thing that the kid had stuck his head out the attic window: Now Pinky knew which room to look in. He'd go back one day this week when no one was home.

Chapter 5

WHEN JULIA WALKED INTO THE KITCHEN at Riverview Farm the next morning at eight o'clock, Finn thought he had never been gladder to see anyone in his whole life. She looked so wonderful that he started to worry right away that she might have removed herself permanently to another world, but it was the old Julia's grin that greeted him.

"Hey, Finny, what's new?" she asked.

Finn could hardly wait to start trying to reveal all that had happened in her absence, but his grandmother bade Julia sit right down and tell them about dance camp. "I'm not going off to the library till I hear if it was as good as you hoped," she said.

"It was perfect," Julia said. Her voice was soft with wonder. "I mean really perfect. I learned so much and I met so many neat people and the dancing was out of this world."

"How about the instruction? Did you have good teachers?"

"The best. Just the best. You should have seen how some of those people dance," she said. "You just wouldn't believe it. We danced hard—it was really hard work—three or four hours a day. And then character class and dance notation and jazz, and we had to keep sewing ribbons on our shoes . . ."

Her face glowed. Finn clenched his jaw.

"Kind of hard to come back to the farm," Gram suggested gently, and Finn felt his heart pause as he waited for Julia's answer.

Julia looked out the window.

"No, not hard. Just different. Mom and Dad asked the same thing. I'm glad to be home—I'd never been away from home for more than a couple of nights—and it's like another world, dancing. I'll always want to dance; I know that now." Her face wore a faraway look, then she turned to them and smiled. "But I'll always want to come home, too. I missed you, both of you—*and all the animals.*" She laughed. "Let's go see them now, Finn."

Finn swallowed. *Well, at least she missed me as much as the animals.* Hearing her talk about that camp, he found himself thinking, *It's as though she really had stepped into another world. I need her back in mine.*

When they went inside the barn, before Julia could get involved with Daisy, Finn grabbed the blackboard that Gram kept there for him and spelled out, LOTS TO TELL YOU.

"Hey, your writing's much better. What's up?"

Finn pointed to the shotgun propped in the corner of the feed room and started to scribble: THEY THINK OUR GUY KILLED A LAMB.

"Oh, the Sanders's lamb. I heard about that last night when I got home." Julia looked at Finn's disturbed expression. "You mean your grandmother is really out to get him?"

Finn nodded.

"Didn't you ever let her know about the trap?" She nodded toward the chalkboard.

Finn shook his head. Then he wrote, YOU TELL.

"Sure, I don't mind, but it won't do much good. Seems like everyone on the hill thinks it was him, Dad said. Seems someone saw him over near the Sanders's farm that day. Whoever it was even said he was limping, so they say it must have been our guy."

Finn groaned.

"I know, if only we could tell them he was too crippled to travel that far. . . . Tell you what, Finn, let me talk to my folks. They listen to me. Sometimes."

Julia picked up a lead line and started for the pasture gate. Finn raised his hand to stop her, to make her see that he was nowhere near through. He had to tell her about the cocaine. But he dropped his hand. *No need to rush*, he thought. He'd show her the cocaine later, maybe keep it one more night. And, taking him by surprise, a little thrill of relief passed through him. *Just one more night . . .*

— ♦ —

As Julia pedaled slowly home, she mulled over the question of the hybrid and decided that they really should talk to Gram about him and get her on their side.

Once that was settled, she allowed her thoughts to return to Finn.

Well, I guess I was crazy to hope he'd be himself again when I got home . . . crazy to think about that kiss so much at camp . . . Why would that have changed anything, dummy?

He probably didn't even think twice about it . . . all he ever thinks about is himself, anyway . . . No, not fair . . . he's too . . . too muffled *to think at all . . . It's like he was somewhere in there, hiding behind a big thick wall, and he's too scared to come out.*

I wonder if he even thought once about that kiss. It felt so . . . so safe. Maybe I'm nuts, but it felt like a kind of promise . . . like he trusted me to help him . . .

Dummy, she told herself again. *You're imagining things.*

But he sure did seem glad to see me this morning. Really glad. I'm glad, too.

She turned onto the narrow dirt road that led to her house. It was so stony and uneven—especially so since the long summer drought—that she dismounted and pushed her bike, hardly noticing the road, intent on the maidenhair fern that grew in such profusion on either side just here.

A neighbor drove by from the opposite direction and, seeing Julia, tooted and braked. She pulled her bike nearly to the ditch and waved, smiling and calling, "Hi," as the neighbor backed toward her. So intent was she on greeting him that she didn't see a tawny shadow slip out of the ditch behind her and cut through the woods toward Riverview Farm.

Toq had been filling his belly with fresh water at a spring he discovered. His wounded foreleg had grown new flesh and hair had begun to cover the ugly scar. The bone itself was still extremely tender, however, forcing him to move awkwardly on three legs. Prey in the wood was scarce and he was still gaunt. The one time he had tried an old hunting ground, halfway across the Sanders's hayfield he'd heard human voices shouting. "There he is! That's him!"

For fear of being seen again, he dared not cross open terrain, but lay day after day in solitude in the brooding shadows of the pinewood, leaving it only for water. Often he sat near the edge of the wood and regarded Riverview Farm and all its inhabitants. Vague intimations stirred and flickered; he did not know what they were, but they troubled him almost as much as his leg. As long as he could remember, Toq had lived in solitude. Now, since the strange boy had released him from the trap, for the first time in his life Toq was lonely.

The next day when Julia went with Finn up to his room to get her backpack, he opened his bureau drawer and showed her the plastic packet of cocaine. She stared at it in amazement.

"Th-that's cocaine, isn't it?"

Finn nodded.

"Y-y-you planning to *use* it?"

Finn flushed. He looked away from her.

"Are you?"

After the slightest pause, Finn shook his head.

"But—but where did you *get* it?"

Finn went to his window and, pulling Julia behind him, pointed toward the pinewood.

"The barn? Oh, no, I see—the pine—oh, my gosh, you mean the *fort*!"

Finn nodded.

"So you just found it there?" Finn pointed to the backpack. "When you went to get my pack?"

Finn nodded again.

"Kids? Like the kids that smoke there . . . some kids at school—"

Finn grabbed her arm again and pointed straight down from his window.

Realization broke over Julia's face like a wash of color.

"Oh—oh—him, under the window. Oh, I bet—it could have been any one of that lot in town . . ."

Finn nodded and reached for a pad of paper and a pencil. This was getting too complicated to communicate by gesture alone.

He wrote as fast as he could, WENT SWIMMING AT RIVER AND SAW THAT MAN. HE MET UP WITH TWO PUSHERS.

Julia paled. She remembered the face of a man who hung out behind the playground at school. There were always a few kids around him; the only one she

knew was a boy named Jack, a couple of grades ahead
of her. The man was a little older, a little pudgy, slop-
ing shoulders . . .

"Did he have reddish hair?" she asked.

Finn nodded.

"Good grief, Finn, this is no joke. If you knew what
goes on in town, you'd freak out over this—"

Vehemently Finn nodded his head.

"It's true what I told Gram, all that talk about
gangs and dope. It started last spring. They even had
meetings at school, and those federal agents are still
down there, Mom says, and—" She paused, a puzzled
expression on her face. "Why did you bring it home?
Why didn't you spell it out for Gram, so she could
report it? Why didn't you just leave it there?"

Finn avoided her eye. He shrugged.

"Listen, Finn, I think we better take this stuff to
the police or something," she said uncertainly. She
stared at the white plastic bag in Finn's hand. "I'm
pretty sure that's what we *should* do, but . . ."

But what if I'm still not ready to give it up? Finn
closed his hand and felt himself blush.

Julia saw it. *He wants to try it,* she thought. *Thinks
it will solve all his problems . . . Oh, Lord . . . But he
didn't try it. He hasn't tried it yet. He waited for me . . .
could that be it? Did he wait for me? I've got to help
him out of this.*

"You know what?" she said. "I think we better just
put it back. We know that man at the window had
something to do with this, Finn. He's mixed up with
kids I go to school with, and I don't want to get them

in trouble. Mostly they're losers, but still . . . I sure don't want anything to do with him or that gang downtown. Let's just put it back and forget our old fort—it doesn't mean anything anymore. If we want to look for him—for the wolf—we can just crawl into the wood some other place."

This suddenly seemed an excellent solution to Finn. All he needed was to hear it said. A wave of relief passed through him, and he smiled at Julia. Yes, he nodded.

"It's already late now. How about tomorrow afternoon, when I come over?"

Finn nodded again. He was sure now that he would pass over the cocaine again tonight.

I was right to wait for Julia, he thought. *Of course we should get rid of this stuff. Tonight I'll play to the stars.*

At eight o'clock that same evening, in the back room of a bar down in the town, cigarette smoke filled the air, stifling the smell of beer. Rafe and Jack sat at a booth with a battered wooden table. Outside, the day had begun to draw in.

"Okay, here's what we're gonna do," said Rafe evenly. "We kept that place for one more drop to see what was what around here, and nothin' happened last Thursday. So maybe Pinky was telling the truth. The other day he tells me he's got a new place even better than the well. I want you to check it out before we make the move."

"Yeah, Rafe, sure. Where is it?" Jack asked uneasily.

He didn't like the direction in which this conversation was headed one bit.

"I'll tell you in a minute," Rafe growled. "But first things first. I don't want to use no new drop of Pinky's till I know for sure if he's into drugs. I just don't trust him no more. If he thinks we believe him, he may get careless. *I gotta know, Jack.* I gotta know, one way or the other, whether to keep Pinky in or throw him out and train some new guy."

Rafe made sure his voice was strong and sure. In no way was Jack to suspect that Pinky had hinted that he knew some things about Rafe he might have to pass on some day. The fact that Pinky was *not* scared scared Rafe more than he would ever admit—to Jack or anyone else. If Pinky ever blew the whistle on Rafe, his cover would be gone for good; he'd be known throughout the whole drug network as a double-dealer, and his colleagues in Mexico City had never been known to let double-dealers live out their natural lives.

"So up till this Thursday, Pinky's still in. But if we—you, Jack—catch him at the drop between now and Thursday, he's outta here next week, when we change drops. And it won't be no drop Pinky knows." Rafe's lip curled. "Yeah, any sign of Pinky messing with my merchandise and he's outta here but good."

Rafe did not inform Jack just what he had in store for Pinky. No sense scaring the punk any more than he already had.

"Okay, so here's the deal: This is Tuesday. Tomorrow

you fix yourself a coupla nice lunches for your lunch box, and you take your sleeping bag and you find someplace outta sight but near the well, and you keep watch. You keep watch on the drop *and* the farm"— Rafe's eyes grew so narrow they almost disappeared under his brooding lashless lids—"and if you fall asleep on watch, you better never let me find you. It's my week on. If nothing's happened by pickup Thursday, I'll relieve you and pick up the goods same as always and we'll all meet here afterward. Then we'll talk about setting up a new drop if I think we need one."

It was nearly full dark by the time Jack settled himself at the southern edge of the pinewood. From there he had a clear view of Riverview Farm as well as of the opening to the path leading up to the well. If anyone came from below, he'd spot them right off. If they came from above, he'd hear them when they entered the wood.

Jack felt awful. He'd had a bad row with his mother about going to a "sleep-over" at a friend's house. Pretending he was mad at her for being so nosy, he wouldn't tell her the friend's name.

This whole thing's crazy, Jack thought to himself. *Just one lie after another. I want out. I'm only a high school junior, and already I seen too much . . . Too many kids are getting sick on this stuff, cops all over the place, school starting soon, Mom pissed off all the time—and, man, what's gonna happen to Pinky?*

I want out. It just ain't worth it.

But, jeez—that Rafe. He don't like me to begin with. If I cut out now . . . Jack felt sick with fright at the thought.

Night fell fully over the valley and with it the special silence of country darkness. It was broken only by the squeals of killdeer in the horse pasture and the thin sweet notes of Finn's recorder.

Lying thirty feet away, Toq laid his muzzle on his paws, never once taking his eyes off the stranger who watched the farm.

Wednesday afternoon Finn waited impatiently for Julia to appear so that they could take the cocaine back up to the old well and be free of it once and for all. For the moment that was his one and only target, taking precedence over everything else in his mind. Dimly he was aware that getting rid of the packet was not the final solution to the rats' nest of troubles they had unearthed, but for him it was the first step out of his own rats' nest. No cocaine, no temptation. *One thing at a time*, he told himself. He had come within an ace of choosing the drug as his route out of himself—such an easy escape it had seemed. But with Julia's return he felt a sense of urgency stirring in him, the first he had felt since the crash. Finn knew, with a shaky certainty, that he wanted to function again. Maybe—yes, probably—he'd even agree to see that shrink Gram had told him about. He could begin by writing things out for the doctor. But first he must get that drug out of his room and off his mind for good.

Impatient, he went down to the barn to wait. The moment he stepped through the door, he felt the coolness of the dim interior; at this hour the sun cast only a short hot block of light onto the floor. All the rest was shadowy and dim. The familiar farm smells and the atmosphere of harmony in the barn soothed his restlessness.

The goats huddled at their gate to greet him, and he stroked their noses. Vetch, demanding as always, butted him again and again until he sparred with her. Then Clover tiptoed up close, her bandaged neck and head making her look like a caricature of a movie queen.

Seeing Belle at the gate, he went over to her and stroked her neck. His right hand no longer wore a glove—the tender new skin looked pink and shiny and there were ridges across the palm. Belle's silvery coat felt like satin under his left hand, but under the right it felt like wool. For a while he scratched and stroked her; then, remembering something Julia had taught him, he raised her chin and breathed into her nostrils.

"That's how you claim a horse," Julia had told him once, when he saw her nose to nose with Daisy. "It bonds you."

Where on earth *was* Julia? Finn glanced at his watch and saw that it was past their usual lunchtime. She ought to be here any second now. Once they got rid of the dope, maybe he'd even go down to the river with her. Maybe even swim.

His eye fell on the ladder to the loft, and he remembered his first morning back at Riverview Farm when he had been unable to climb it. Encouraged by the new mobility his lightweight cast gave him, he put his good foot on the first rung. Clasping the rails on either side hurt his right hand, so he concentrated on the left one as a pulley and mounted slowly rung by rung.

Just as he reached out to unlatch the hook at the top, Julia walked in the lower level and called out, "Finn?"

Finn half turned. His right hand slipped off the rung. For a split second he teetered wildly, his right arm flailing, the left reaching too late for the rail. Then he slid straight down the ladder, bumping the side of his head on each rung along the way. He heard the cast smash as he hit the floor.

As it was Wednesday, Gram was home. She drove Finn and Julia to the hospital, where the doctor pronounced him to be all in one piece, despite bruises and abrasions to his face and ribs. Finn ached all over. He had to bite his lip when the new cast was fitted.

"All in all, I'd say you're a very lucky young man," said the doctor kindly. Finn ground his teeth. "You haven't rebroken the ankle. The hand will hurt for a day or two, but you haven't done it any serious harm, and that old scar on your face should be pretty near gone in a few weeks." He touched the new scrapes and said, "These will heal in no time. Just try to stay in one piece until school starts, okay, Finn?" The doctor smiled.

"I'm supposed to go to Montpelier tomorrow to do some paperwork for the library. Should I cancel?" asked Finn's grandmother.

"This won't set him back. Just keep him quiet today, then he can do whatever he feels up to, which won't be much for a few days."

Finn was plunged in gloom. He sat in the backseat of Gram's car on the way home, scowling out the window. No matter what Julia said, he would not look at her or smile. Just as he was getting better, this had to happen. Now, he and Julia would not be able to get rid of the cocaine today. He knew he'd never make it up through the pinewood feeling like this.

Why was it that every time he began to feel the smallest whiff of hope, something set him back? Was he meant to live like this for the rest of his life? Out of the blue the slick white pouch lying in his bureau drawer appeared in his mind's eye and he pounced upon it. Maybe this was a sign. Maybe he was *meant* to take that cocaine. The thought turned him sour; this was not what he'd had in mind this morning when he thought about living a real life again.

The closer they got to home, the worse grew his mood. His grandmother turned onto the long narrow dirt road leading up from the valley toward the farm. Just as they rumbled across the little wooden bridge over a brook, a sudden movement caught Finn's eye.

"Look!" Julia cried.

But Finn had already seen what Julia saw—right there, just to the right of the car: a blurred motion of fur, tail straight out, head down, as the wolf-dog rose up from drinking in the brook and disappeared into the undergrowth. Even in that brief half second, Finn could see his gait was flawed.

"I saw him," said Finn's grandmother. "He's something else, all right, isn't he? Looks hurt. Maybe somebody took a shot at him. You know, it's a funny thing, but I'm rather glad they missed."

Julia glanced at Finn as though to ask, *"Shall we?"* He merely shrugged, so Julia said, "No, he got caught in a trap up in the pinewood, near the fort. We found him the first day we went up there. We let him loose," she finished lamely.

Finn's grandmother slowed to make the turn into her lane.

"Why didn't you tell me?" she asked, glancing at Finn in the rearview mirror.

He refused to return her look.

"Well, we knew you thought he attacked Clover and—"

"And you don't."

"No, Gram, we don't. I talked to my parents about it last night and they say we could be right. Seems coyotes had been seen and heard up near Sanders's place, too, right about the time they lost that lamb. Anyway, we were going to tell you about it, but then Finn fell down the ladder and . . ."

"Well, you know, now that I see him again, up close,

I don't either, really, though I don't know why. Not just because he's lame—there's something about him. Anyway, I'm not going to shoot that animal myself," said Gram. "I just wish you two had let me in on the story about finding him in a trap. That's quite an adventure."

She drove past the barn and drew up at the kitchen door.

"Now, Finny, here we are home again, and it's half past three and no one's had any lunch. Julia, come on in and we'll fix something to eat—then perhaps our wounded soldier will lie down for a while."

She turned to smile at Finn, but he simply slammed the car door behind him and limped into the house.

His thirst sated, Toq limped back to his den and lay down, panting lightly while the long summer afternoon turned to evening. The night before he had caught a rabbit—quite a rarity in these parts—and for the first time since getting caught in the trap his belly was full. As soon as it was darker, he would weave his way through the pinewood and lie hidden, nearer to where the strange man sat, just inside the edge of the trees. Just sitting there hour after hour, dozing and watching, dozing and watching.

He rested for a while, then crawled on his belly to within feet of the intruder.

Julia knocked on Finn's half-open door and entered without waiting for a sign.

"Your grandmother said for you to take this—

doctor's orders," she said to the back of his head.

Finn turned and glowered at her. Ignoring him, she walked over to his window and turned on the fan Gram had bought when the heat refused to lift. Then she sat down on the edge of his bed and handed over two tablets and a glass of water.

"Here. It's some kind of painkiller. She sent me so you wouldn't bite her head off."

Finn rolled onto his back and elbowed his way to a half-sitting position. Every bone in his body ached, his hand burned, and his whole face felt raw. Still scowling, he accepted the pills and drank them down.

"She says they'll help you to sleep," Julia said, and Finn snorted. Sleep! That was the last thing he wanted to do. He had much too much on his mind to sleep. Besides, his sentries were too sore to stand guard.

Julia lowered her voice. "Maybe we should just tell her and let her decide what to do?"

Trust Julia to suggest something sensible, thought Finn sourly. Half-furious over the mounting pile of setbacks to his life and half desperate to overcome them, he shook his head violently. *No.*

"Do you want me to take it back now, before I go home? It's still plenty light out."

Again Finn shook his head.

"You want me to wait for you?"

Finn nodded, agitated. He couldn't get a handle on all these questions. Too many things were piling up in his head, like those clouds over the Absarokas, but that packet of cocaine was his business now. He just needed to stop hurting so much; he just needed a little more time, some rest. Then maybe he could write it out for her.

"Okay. I understand."

Finn lay back and stared at the ceiling. *Maybe she does,* he thought. *I think maybe she does.*

For a few seconds Julia watched him without saying a word. She studied his face intently, surer than ever that Finn feared the cocaine for reasons that had nothing to do with the law or his grandmother or the wolf-dog.

"Finn, listen to me," she said. "Sleep now." He turned his head and frowned at her. "Well, rest at least. Here's what we'll do tomorrow. It's Thursday and your grandmother's leaving in the morning to go to Montpelier for the library. And I have to go to town for a dentist appointment. I'll come over as soon as I get back, but don't expect me till around two o'clock. Maybe you'll be up to going to the fort by then. We'll go together—you'll see, we'll manage to get rid of that dope." Julia drew a breath and spoke without knowing what she was going to say. "Then we can get to work making you whole again."

She picked up *Catcher in the Rye*, lying facedown on the floor by his bed, and began to read aloud.

Half an hour later, looking up from the page, Julia saw that the day was over. Finn had fallen fast asleep. His face looked so tender and unarmed, so free of pain and worry, that she almost dreaded having him wake up.

What if he's too sore to take that stupid cocaine up tomorrow? It'll just torture him for another whole day.

Inaction frustrated Julia, who liked to deal with life head-on as it unfolded. The idea of Finn agonizing over the cocaine on top of everything else seemed both unfair and unnecessary to her.

What can I do? she wondered. And out of the dim still room an idea came to her like a lightbulb turning on.

But of course! I'll take it up, and then it will be over and done with. He'll be glad tomorrow when he knows it's over. I'll take it up as soon as day breaks— the plan unfolded neatly—*I'll leave my bike behind the tool shed, so nobody will know.*

With a rush of relief, she crossed the little room to his bureau, opened the top drawer, and slipped the packet of cocaine into the pocket of her jeans.

It was cold in the Absarokas. Bitter cold, even at the very end of May. Snow lay in pockets on the highlands, the earth was winter brown, and each time wind stirred, the cold sliced through him like a knife. At some point his body simply gave in to it and tuned out.

He woke at dawn to a tranquil blue sky. Right away he saw the four coyotes watching him, but his body seemed to be paralyzed, so he just stared back at the one nearest him. After what seemed quite a long time it occurred to him that he was literally frozen stiff. He managed to sit forward a little and tried to beat himself with his arms to scare the coyotes away and make the blood move, but his right hand flamed with pain. He looked at it, surprised; it was a mess—

charred and raw. He could even see the muscles.

His hand frightened him and he tried to rise. The movement sent a shock of pain from his ankle; it traveled up his shin to the knee, gripping the leg so fiercely that he almost passed out. He lay back against the boulder and the pain ebbed. Almost immediately he became aware of the cold again and began to shiver until his teeth rattled, causing the coyote nearest him to move back a few feet.

When he put his left hand up to hold the chattering jaw, he discovered that a piece of his face was missing. There was a long wound from his forehead across his cheek. Somehow or other it had missed the eye. He could see. He closed the other eye and he could still see. That was something. The bleeding on his face must have stopped; his fingers came away wet, but not with blood, so he knew he must be weeping. Unwilling to take in any more information, he closed his eyes and drifted back into a kind of sleep . . .

During the next couple of hours the sun rose in the wide Wyoming sky, warming Finn enough to thaw his body. He regained consciousness and in one searing moment recognized the terribleness of his predicament. Then something even more terrible happened: Panic hit him with the force of a fist. Unfocused, irrational, all-powerful—worst of all, he had no name for this mindless terror, no hook to hang it on so that he could stand aside and study the fear.

He heard grunting noises and realized they came from his throat. He must run . . . He must run before this wave of terror washed him over an unthinkable *edge and he cracked into a million pieces. Gasping for breath, he struggled once again to rise to his feet. Immediately the left leg crumpled and he fell against the boulder. The pain flooded his body; it seemed to take the place of blood, driving out any other perception and bringing him to his senses. Thankfully Finn almost welcomed it.*

The coyotes had retreated several paces when he rose. Now they sat back on their haunches, watching him. Their tilted eyes were yellow; steam rose from the long pink tongues hanging from their mouths. Finn stared back at them, panting. But he did not really see them. All his attention was focused on his ankle. He knew he would have to move the leg again to relieve the ferocity of that pain. In the meantime he let the pain take over and ride through him.

When he was ready, when he knew the limits of the pain, he slowly shifted his weight from one side to the other. Keeping his eyes fixed on the lead coyote, he became aware of the rhythm of its breath—a regular light pant—and he adusted his own breathing to match. This gave him something to concentrate on while he resettled his body and allowed it to plunge gratefully into unconsciousness.

It was afternoon when he came to. The moment he opened his eyes, the terror smote him again. This time he found hook after hook to hang it on as the blood roared louder and louder in his ears.

When will they start to look for me? Will they look for me?

How will they ever find me? Uncle Matt—he knows this country as well as Dad.

Dad. But Dad is dead. Will Uncle Matt come instead?

No, no, no . . . No one will find me.

If I hadn't jumped—if I'd got there faster, caught Dad's hand. If only . . . I might have saved them . . .

Thin plumes of smoke still rose from the wreck. His father's hand, black but perfectly formed, hung still from the open door. A terrible new thought pierced Finn's head: When the embers of the plane had cooled, the coyotes would eat the remains of his family. They would start with the hand.

Once again he heard the animal noise in his throat; once again he retreated into unconsciousness.

He woke to find the sun almost sunk behind the range. Three coyotes had inched closer. One sniffed at Finn's foot. Wisps of smoke still tainted the air. Finn turned to look at the plane and saw the other coyote take his father's hand between its teeth. *Oh, no, no, no!* Even as he mouthed the words, the coyote, repulsed by the heat, backed off and came to rejoin the others.

Then, from somewhere out of the enormous silence, came the sound of a small plane's engine. Hope exploded in Finn's heart. He leaned forward and saw a glint of light on metal far to the west.

"Here!" he tried to cry, daring to wave his arm.

But the tiny plane droned on. Finn watched it disappear into the deepening sky.

The moment he knew for sure that no one had seen

him, the panic began to gather again, like the dark thickening all around him, and cold dulled his body's pain, so that he lost his one weapon against the fear.

It's all over now, he said to himself. There is nothing I can do. I am helpless. I will die and the coyotes will live. In the last of the twilight he saw the steam of the lead coyote's breath. It rose in even little puffs from the sharp gray muzzle. Finn's eyes fastened on the steam; over the roar in his ears he heard the light panting sound. His mind turned transparent and again he began to breathe in the same rhythm as the coyote.

Later he had no idea how long he lay breathing with the coyote. Time was meaningless in a strange familiar place that felt more like home than any house where he had ever lived. No walls. Just a space and he deep in the invisible center. Here. Here I am.

Help me, Finn cried silently.

Help me, he said again and again.

It was the raucous rattle of the heliocopter blades that next dragged him back to consciousness. He opened his eyes to sunrise once again. The helicopter had landed on a little shelf of land not a hundred yards from where he lay. Two men were climbing down from the cockpit. The coyotes were gone.

Finn began to sob. There were no tears and the sound he made was raw and ugly to his ears. But he thought his heart would burst with gratefulness.

Chapter 6

THURSDAY DAWNED SLOWLY, heavy with heat. In times of drought the valley farms often survived better than those along the hillsides, because the heavy August dew took partial place of water. But Riverview Farm lay a little too high to profit from the moisture, so that, except for Ben's grave, the horse pasture was cropped close and nearly brown. Even the great maples on the lawn seemed to pale and sag with heat.

The four horses, the goats, the five fat hens all stayed under cover later than usual, drugged by the oppressive air. Only Belle heard the sound of a bicycle in the lane. She moved out into the barnyard and peered around the corner facing the road.

Julia, dismounting, looked surprised to see her.

"Well, for heaven's sake," she whispered. "What good ears you have, for an old lady."

Lifting the mare's delicate nose to her own, she breathed into it.

"Dear old friend," she murmured, stroking Belle's throat. "Oh, my, your heart's going like a leaky old outboard. Must be this weather, poor Belle. Here"—and she led the mare back into the shadow of the shed— "it's a little cooler here. You stay in the shade and take care of things till I get back."

Even though the sun had not fully risen, Julia was sweating by the time she entered the pinewood. It was still dark in there, dark and quiet. No crickets. No birdsong. Just the faint shuffling sound of her sneakers as she climbed up the familiar path of needles. She could see that Finn had cleared it a lot while she was gone. Julia walked upright, her compact dancer's body moving rapidly up the slope. From time to time she fingered the packet of cocaine in her pocket.

She was quite pleased with herself. Surely this was best for Finn. Everything had fallen into place just as planned. Before leaving the previous evening, she and Finn's grandmother had synchronized their schedules for today: Gram would leave for Montpelier at ten, putting Finn's lunch and a short list of easy chores for him on the kitchen table.

Julia had explained that her mother wanted her to look for school clothes—Julia always checked out the stores on her own before she and her mother shopped together. And then, at 12:45, she had a dentist's appointment, so probably it would be nearly two o'clock before she got to Riverview Farm. But Gram needn't worry: She'd stay with Finn until his grandmother returned later in the afternoon. In fact, she'd see to it that supper was started for the three of them.

Slipping away from home before dawn this morning in order to unload the packet presented no problem at all. Dad would be gone to work by now, and on Tuesdays and Thursdays her mother went to her own job in the next town. If for any reason her mother noticed Julia's absence and mentioned it when she got home tonight, Julia would simply say she had stayed out in their barn after chores, doing her dance exercises at the barre. She often practiced early, so as to keep the afternoons free for Finn.

Halfway to the fort Julia paused to flap the T-shirt stuck to her torso. *When Mom and I go shopping later this week, we'd better get some new ones,* she thought. That reminded her of the sandals she had seen downtown. Mom would put up a fuss when she saw them— too expensive, she'd say, and too impractical. Who'd want to wear outlandish sandals like that? she'd ask.

Me, said Julia to herself, and grinned. *They were really cool.*

Tugging at the neck of the T-shirt, she blew down her front. Her skin was speckled with pine dust. Julia could hardly wait to get home and shower before biking into town. She took a step forward and then she froze. There on the path before her stood the hybrid. He almost looked as though he were trying to scare her away.

Toq had spent the entire night awake, his eyes fixed on the intruder. Just once he had backed away when the man lit a cigarette. Toq hated the smell of tobacco smoke. Instinctively it filled him with dread. Where there's smoke there's fire, Toq knew.

How long would the stranger stay on watch? Was he one of those whom Toq had seen cross the heifer pasture late at night? No way to tell for sure, he was upwind of the man. Toq was tired and thirsty, but he could not drag himself away. Hidden deep in the shadow of the trees, he kept glancing down at the house and barn as they emerged from the darkness of night. Suddenly he stiffened.

There, just east of the barn, someone was crossing the pasture. The girl; it was the girl. Toq rose to his three feet. At the same moment he heard a crashing sound above. Something was moving through the pines up there. The stranger heard it, too. Toq saw him roll to his hands and knees and begin to move quickly along the edge of trees to the path, where he turned and disappeared from Toq's sight.

Toq hesitated, poised to flee the wood entirely. But that girl . . . Following an instinct he did not understand, Toq hastened under the web of branches and arrived at the edge of the path just as Julia entered the wood and started for the fort. He saw her before she saw him. Sheltered by the dense growth, he waited while she paused to cool herself. Then he moved into the center of the path to block her way.

Jack, every nerve strung tight, crawled toward the fort. He had heard nothing more since the sound of breaking twigs moments before. The air deep in the pinewood was thick, the light gray. *Thunderstorm weather*, Jack thought. From the well came the faint sound of stones rattling.

Let it be a deer, he prayed, as he crept agonizingly slowly under the dead, tinder-dry branches. *Oh, please let it be a deer.*

But he knew with a clarity beyond his years that it was not a deer up there near the fort; and as he inched his way over a low rise of the forest floor and glimpsed the clearing around the springhouse, his heart sank.

No. Not a deer. Pinky.

Pinky let the door of his pickup swing shut and made his way across the deserted heifer pasture to the trail. He felt the dregs of his last hit seeping out of him, but his mood was very nearly euphoric. He had the whole day in front of him to fix this week's delivery, and once he'd had his first snort, he had the whole day to enjoy the fruits of his labors at leisure.

No need to fear running into Rafe at this hour. Now that nothing bad had happened as a result of his trip to Riverview Farm, there was no need to fear Rafe at all anymore. He congratulated himself. He almost wished he had an excuse to confront Rafe with the evidence. Well, maybe that wasn't such a red-hot idea. No point inflaming Rafe just yet. Better let the narcs do that, if push came to shove.

In the half-light of dawn he tripped going over the stone wall, crashing through a tangle of branches as he fell to his knees. He almost laughed.

Clumsy old me, he said to himself affectionately. *Nearly there.*

When he reached the well, he squatted and felt along the stones of the wall for the magic one that opened the drop. The gloomy day had continued to lighten reluctantly, so that even in the dark and airless pinewood he could see the treasure when he pulled the stone aside: a bulging leather bag. Pinky grinned and went straight to work.

With a great effort he controlled the tremors that were beginning in his hands. Carefully he opened ten of the little plastic bags and dumped half the powder into another one he drew from his pocket. The other half he poured into a second bag in which he had already mixed his own combination of what the trade called junk. Shaking it thoroughly, he began to pour the altered drug back into the ten packets, tying each one neatly as they filled.

Halfway through he stiffened. Head cocked, he strained to hear what he thought, but could not believe, he had heard: footsteps mounting the path.

Kee-rist, someone's in the wood! Someone's coming straight for the drop. Rafe. Jeezus, it's Rafe. He's using the other path.

At the very thought of Rafe, Pinky panicked. The tremors increased. He scrambled together all the packets and all the powder, pure and cut, into the leather pouch and lurched to his feet.

What to do? If Rafe caught him in the act, forget

the evidence. The jig was up for sure. Better let him think they had been robbed. Shoving the bulging sack into his shirtfront, Pinky stepped as far back as possible into the dense undergrowth and flung himself facedown on the forest floor. Hurriedly he scooped pine needles over his most exposed parts and lay there, holding his breath.

A new sound wafted through the wood. A voice—not Rafe's . . . He let out his breath . . . A female voice . . . was that possible? Only one voice . . . talking to whom? . . . Maybe the mute? *By God, I'll make him sorry he ever stole my dope.*

Pinky's spirits lifted. One after the other, plans of action careened through his jumbled mind. Forcing himself to take silent shallow breaths, he lowered his head, pulled his shirt up over his face and, no longer terrified, waited for whatever came up the path. Then he'd have his snort.

Far above him, as dawn turned to day, a red-winged blackbird trilled.

"Hello," Julia breathed

She could hardly believe her eyes. There he stood, right in front of her on the path. Every feature of the wolf-dog was clear to her: the fine wide head, the deep-set eyes, the heavy coat and massive chest.

Julia sat on her heels and held out one hand. Toq did not move. She saw confusion in his eyes, and a touch of alarm, but he stood his ground. Julia inched forward on her haunches, reaching to stroke him. But this was more than Toq could handle. He backed away from her.

"No?" Julia asked softly. "Okay. I have to go now, but I'll come back for you. I'll bring Finn. We'll meet you here, you'll see." She thought of the time she had spent in Finn's room last night and of the unspoken sense of trust between them. Her heart bursting with happiness, she rose and strode purposefully up the path. Toq moved aside to let her pass and melted back into the woods.

When Julia got to the fort, she stopped again to flap her shirt and wipe her brow with the back of one arm. *Whew, it's going to be a humdinger. But what a great start to the day! That animal! Finn would flip out.* Now all she had to do was get rid of this scary packet, and they were home free.

She looked around for a likely place to leave the cocaine. Remembering how her backpack had ended up almost invisible at the bottom of the well, Julia decided to leave it on the ground near the base. The shiny white square would show up against the dark pine needles, make it easier for those crazy, dumb kids to find.

Her eye fell on the hole in the base of the wall. Curious, she knelt down to investigate it. Just as her hand reached in to explore the cavity, she heard a noise and turned in time to glimpse a figure rising up from the other side of the well. She gasped.

Him. The one dealing at the high school. The one under Finn's window. She opened her mouth to cry out, but in one stride the man was beside her. Without a word he picked Julia up in his two hands, raised her to the top of the wall, and dropped her into the well.

Jack, watching bug-eyed from his hiding place, stifled a gasp of disbelief. Then, taking advantage of Pinky's attention to the girl, he twisted himself around on his stomach and, rising to all fours, half ran, half crawled back down the slope of the pinewood.

Gotta get to Rafe, he panted to himself. *Ain't no other way, now.*

Through a groggy haze Finn had heard the door shut quietly behind Julia when she left his room Wednesday evening. He hovered for a while on the edge of sleep, half resenting his grandmother for giving him the pills, half luxuriating in the rest they gave his tired body.

His mind, too, was relaxed. It didn't resist the flood of memories of those last two days in the mountains. Finn walked through them step-by-step. After the heliocopter it was easier: the ride to Cody; the arrival of Gram; the hours of pain in the hospital; the memorial service at West Thumb; the long plane ride east, ending here at Riverview Farm.

He opened one eye and saw that the window was black, so it must be pretty late. Turning onto his side made him wince. His leg still hurt; in fact, his whole body was stiff. If it was that dark outside, perhaps he would sleep just a little longer.

When finally Finn awoke, a thick light filled the

room. Something important was supposed to happen today. Had he missed it? He lay still, trying to guess the hour and orient himself. Usually he could pinpoint the time within minutes, but today the light was queer, neither sunlight nor cloud. The air was heavier than usual for early morning, further confusing him, so Finn reached for his watch and saw it was 6:45. Then he remembered the cocaine and his and Julia's plan. That was it. No problem. They weren't going to take it back until this afternoon. He felt light with relief at the thought.

Gingerly, he put his foot with the new cast on the floor. So far, so good; the leg ached, but that was to be expected. When he set the other foot down and stood up, however, he grunted with pain. His body must have taken some beating when he fell. Perhaps a shower would help loosen him up and make the trek to the fort easier. Painfully, he limped to the bathroom, reaching with his good hand for support from the walls all along the way.

Finn's grandmother looked up from her library report when he entered the kitchen. Her hair was uncombed and she still wore barn boots. He could see her obviously erasing any trace of worry from her face and was immediately annoyed.

"Pretty stiff?" she asked.

He shrugged one shoulder, shook his head, and sat down in the rocker. Every muscle shrieked as he lowered his weight, but Finn simply stared out the window.

Damn, but he was sore.

— ✦ —

Julia could not believe what had happened to her. At first her mind simply refused to accept as fact that another human being had picked her up and thrown her down the well. Huddled on the stony bottom, she heard him moving around the base of the wall—an occasional grunt, stones rattling—small sounds, invisible but near at hand.

Then no sound at all. Silence, broken only by the noise of insects in the well disturbed by her fall.

She felt herself all over and found her body was in one piece. Only her watch was broken, smashed on the stones. In slow motion, her stunned mind began to function.

Why? Why? Why?

Then, with a little gasp: *Oh, no! Can it—Is it—Is this, this . . . the pushers' drop?*

Julia went cold with shock. Somehow the idea of teenagers using this place as a hangout had not surprised her. After all, she and Finn and Penny used to come here to sneak cigarettes. But it was for kids. It was a great hiding place from grown-ups, nothing more—a playhouse for kids.

In the ominous silence outside her prison Julia's thoughts moved on: The hole in the wall was empty, she was sure of that. So she must have caught him in the act of putting in or taking out. Money? Drugs?

And then a terrible thought brought her mind to a halt and she felt a prickle of gooseflesh rising on her arms.

He must know that I saw him. He must know that.

From years of watching TV and reading mystery novels Julia knew that witnesses to crime were doomed. Little ripples of panic made her face tingle. Her hand closed around the packet in her pocket. What if he knew she had cocaine? Could she use that as bait to set her free?

But is he still here?

Silence.

Has he gone? Why? Where? Has he gone to fetch another pusher?—at the thought she gave a little moan of fright—*or is he still out there, waiting? Just waiting for me to move first?*

She held her breath the better to hear over the rapid drumbeat of her heart.

Silence. No sound of him, no sound at all.

Okay. He's gone.

Julia swallowed, but her mouth was so dry nothing went down. She stood up and began to examine her prison closely—its rough stone walls and the open circular top, so near and yet so far away. *It can't be more than nine or ten feet. I ought to be able to handle that.*

Mossy rocks protruded here and there, she noted. Her spirits rose.

Good. Handholds, that'll help.

She backed against the wall and flung herself at the opposite side of the well, reaching for the extended stones and missing them by inches. Falling back, she felt the first signs of real panic. Quickly she suppressed them, rose, and tried again. Again she failed.

This time she lay quietly on the uncomfortable

bottom, clenching her jaw to stem the tide of claustrophobia gathering in the pit of her stomach.

Stop, she told herself. *Stop. Rest a bit. No need to hurry. He's gone. Rest a bit longer and try again.*

Jack braked his pickup to a stop outside Rafe's boardinghouse on River Street. He glanced at his watch. 6:45. Rafe was going to be mad at being woken up, but nowhere near as mad as he'd be if Jack didn't tell him what Pinky—that damn *fool* Pinky—had done.

Stealing the drug was bad enough, but throwing Julia in the well—Jee*zus*. Rafe was going to have to figure out how to get Julia out. No way Jack could leave her there. He'd do it Rafe's way, but somebody had to get Julia out of that well. And then—what the *hell* was Rafe gonna do to Pinky?

Jack groaned. He didn't have much use for Pinky, but he sure didn't like ratting on him, either. For better or worse, they were in this together. When Jack began to suspect that Pinky was the one messing with the merchandise, he put the thought aside. Maybe it wasn't true. It was up to Rafe to figure it out.

Jack saw a kid coming down the sidewalk with a dog on a leash. He waited until the kid passed, then opened the pickup door, closed it quietly behind him and walked quickly up the steps of the boardinghouse porch.

Pinky replaced the stone over the opening and crawled out of the clearing to his hiding place under the pine boughs. His hands were shaking so hard that he had trouble opening the neck of the leather pouch.

God Almighty, he whimpered to himself, scuffling through the packets of white powder as they fell onto the pine needles and spilled their contents. *Gotta snort, then I'll figure out what to do with her.*

His hand hovered over the bags. Which was which? Oh, jeez, *which was which?*

Frantically he pawed through the plastic bags. One after another he picked them up and squinted at the tops to see if he could recognize the difference in the way they were tied. No use. The shakes had come upon him so fiercely that he could barely hold on to a packet.

Can't wait, he mumbled. *Gotta have a fix. Half this stuff's okay—okay, lady luck, here we go . . .*

Staring out the kitchen window, Finn could see that even the twins looked bedraggled from the sullen, heavy day. The other goats lay despondently in the shade of the barn. No sign of the horses—they must still be in the shed.

"Breakfast?" asked his grandmother.

He gathered himself to rise from the rocker, but his whole body recoiled from the pain. *Damn,* he thought and scowled.

Gram put a bowl of cold cereal in his hands and poured on some milk.

"Raspberries," she said and sprinkled a few over the cereal. "Now, Finny, you know I have to leave for

Montpelier this morning. Too bad, because it's such an awful day. I can hardly breathe, it's so humid. The only good thing about it is there's bound to be a storm later and heaven knows we need the rain."

She returned to the table and took up her report. "I've got to finish this before I go, but I left some egg salad in the fridge for your lunch and I made a pitcher of iced tea. If you get bored just sitting around, there's a list of chores on the blackboard. Julia said she'd be over around two. You could help her fix supper."

Finn ate the cereal and set the bowl on the floor. He stayed in the rocker, leafing through a pile of old magazines that sat on the windowsill. He wished he'd remembered to bring down *Catcher* because he couldn't remember where Julia had been when he'd fallen asleep, but he knew he was near enough the end to finish the book before she came over. The thought of climbing back up to the attic to fetch it was just too much, though.

Gram got up and left the room. Finn heard her go upstairs. When she came down again, her hair was combed into a neat bun on top of her head and she had on her Sunday shoes.

"Thought you might want this," she said, laying *Catcher in the Rye* on his lap.

Finn looked up at her. The handsome, weather-beaten face with its dark brows and halo of gray hair touched his heart in a rush of half-forgotten love. He smiled at his grandmother, openly, then took her rough old hand and laid it against his cheek.

Hurriedly she leaned over and kissed the top of his head; blinking, she turned away and gathered up her report and her purse.

"'Bye, Finny. See you around four. Don't forget to shut the windows if it rains."

When the car engine started, Finn thought, *It's a good thing Julia's coming—I don't know if I'd make it up that hill without her. Oh, well, we'll see. Six more hours . . . maybe I'll feel better by then.*

He picked up *Catcher* and lost himself in Holden Caulfield's dilemmas and dreams.

Jack knocked nervously on Rafe's door. Nothing happened. He looked at his watch again. Getting on for seven—Rafe was just going to have to wake up. Jack knocked again. Still no answer.

Jeez, Rafe's gonna kill me, Jack thought, rehearsing again how he'd tell Rafe what happened at the drop.

He turned the handle and found to his surprise that the door was not locked. With the words already formed and on the tip of his tongue, Jack stepped into the room. But—and Jack could hardly believe his eyes—Rafe wasn't there. The bed was empty and unmade. The room itself felt empty through and through. Jack turned and headed back down the stairs.

Breakfast, he said to himself. *He'll be at the diner having breakfast.* But when he swung through the blurred glass door of the diner, he saw immediately that Rafe wasn't there. Three regulars sat at a booth over coffee.

"Anyone seen Rafe?" Jack asked. He knew no one was supposed to connect him to Rafe, and he knew no one in town liked Rafe, even the users, but time was running out.

The three men looked at one another.

"Ronnie here said he saw him last night," said one.

"Yeah?" said Jack. He waited, but no one said anything more. "Where?"

"Seems like he was headed for Ludlow," said Ronnie.

Ludlow! Jack groaned inwardly. Another half hour gone and no way of knowing for sure if Rafe would be there. He raised his hand in a wave and left the diner. Driving to Ludlow, Jack tried to remember exactly where the drug ring's hangout was.

Hours passed. How many, Julia could not guess. When all her efforts to escape had failed and there was no further sign or sound from her abductor, she had finally slipped into a fitful sleep, in hopes that somehow Finn would find her.

Suddenly a branch snapped and something moved slowly and clumsily outside the well. She sat up, disoriented and terrified.

"Who's that?" Julia cried, but no one answered.

She rolled her body into a tight circle, tucking her head between her knees.

If he thinks I haven't seen his face, he'll think

I can't tell, she told herself fiercely.

Julia strained to hear footsteps, breath, anything she could identify. From somewhere quite nearby she heard retching and a low moan. Then silence, total heavy silence. Minute followed minute. Nothing stirred, not even the insects in the well.

And suddenly Julia's aloneness was more than she could bear. Anything was better than being left to rot in this well. She lurched to her feet.

"Help me, help me out!" she cried.

She flung herself high against the inner wall of the well, but her toes still could find no niche to hold them and she fell back onto the needle-strewn rocky bottom.

"Who are you? What do you want? Just tell me what you want—I won't tell a soul. I don't know you, I won't look at you, just tell me what you want!" Her voice was high with fright and she started to weep.

Pinky, curled on his side in the clearing, listened through a thickening fog to her cries. He remembered starting back to the well with some purpose in mind. It had to do with Rafe, impressing Rafe. Was it today? Yesterday? Halfway there the drug overtook him with the force of a hammer blow. He staggered the last few paces through the web of branches and fell forward, his heart racing, nausea swirling through his belly.

God, I've snorted the junk. He knew it. His stomach rose up to his gullet and he vomited. That helped some. He fumbled a cigarette from the pocket of his jeans and lit it. The smoke filled his lungs and shocked his system into a momentary burst of energy. Fingers shaking, nose running, stomach starting to stir again, he took another drag.

Julia smelled the smoke. *So he is still there*, she thought. She bit her lip to stop from crying and with a mighty effort forced herself to think. The bindles! Of course, how could she have forgotten?

"I have a present for you," she called softly. "A nice plastic bag full of cocaine. You help me out and you get the whole thing and I won't say a word. You can even tie something over my eyes—"

"Where'd you get it?"

"Found it. Found it here at the well."

His cocaine, by God! Hope exploded in Pinky. That was pure stuff—pure, sure stuff. *That'll fix me up*, he almost sang to himself.

He started to crawl to the well, but the need to vomit again overwhelmed him and some vestige of modesty made him turn away out of the girl's hearing. He made it to the edge of the clearing, threw up, and collapsed. The last thing he remembered before losing consciousness was the smell of smoke as his cigarette rolled into the needles.

Chapter 7

FINN READ ON AND ON. Because there were aspects of Salinger's hero that reminded him of his present self, the long hot midday passed more quickly than he had hoped. Bit by bit the sky darkened and Finn grew aware of distant thunder, but he was engrossed in his book and only laid it aside to eat the egg salad and drink the iced tea. His grandmother made the best iced tea Finn had ever tasted. Even his mother's wasn't quite as good, though she'd learned from Gram.

The taste of tea and lemon on his tongue reminded him vividly of his mother, back in Wyoming, welcoming him home from school. She wore denim overalls and her long dark hair hung in a braid down her back. She held out a pitcher of tea and—Finn started to shut down the image, but suddenly changed his mind. He let her in. He let her come right into the kitchen. His mother smiled her warm, wide smile. Tears came to Finn's eyes and they felt good. Was she really here? Or was it only memory? Did it matter? The thing was, he had let her in, and she had smiled. For now, that was enough.

When he limped back to the rocker, the aches and pains in his body returned him to the present and reminded him of the task at hand. The pain was pretty near as bad as it was in the Absarokas—well, not really, but still, he did hurt. Just how was he going to make it up that path? Maybe he'd only go as far as the gate to the pinewood with Julia and wait for her there. But no, something in Finn was determined. It had to do with that issue of control: He would return that cocaine himself and then decide what came next.

The storm was approaching and the thunder, though still muted, came more frequently. By a quarter to two Finn had to turn on the light so he could go on reading, but he soon laid the book aside. Restless, he checked the time again.

Hurry up, Julia, he thought. *We don't want to get caught in this storm.*

He stood up and forced himself to walk back and forth in the kitchen in hopes of limbering up his stiff muscles. When his grandmother's aged clock rasped dully twice, Finn sighed with relief and moved to the open door expectantly. No sign of Julia yet.

There's nothing to worry about—Julia's always on time. She'll be here any minute, he said to himself.

And once again, as it had so many times this summer, his heart felt a little flush of comfort at the thought of her.

— ✦ —

It must be getting on for two, she told herself fiercely.

Julia had no idea how long it had been since the man stopped moving.

If I don't show up at two, Finn's going to wonder where I am.

Then what? her frightened self asked. *He can't call the dentist, can't call his grandmother, can't call for help at all.*

He'll—she faltered—*he'll what? If he goes upstairs, he might open his drawer and then he'll see the cocaine is gone, then he'll guess. If. If he goes down to the barn, he might go 'round the other side of the toolshed and see my bike and guess. If.*

But what if he's too stiff to do either one? moaned the other self.

Somebody *will figure it out. Finn will find a way to tell somebody I'm missing.*

Julia chewed the inside of her cheek to stop herself from crying. So intent was she on holding herself together that she did not at first smell the wisps of smoke from Pinky's burning cigarette.

The minutes ticked slowly by. Inch by inch, invisibly, little tongues of fire began to move under the heavy carpet of pine needles. The only trace of the fire's progress was a thin veil of smoke rising here and there from the forest floor.

Finn frowned. Where could she be? Quarter past two, and still no Julia? It was unheard of. He knew her dentist's name, but could not call. Neither of Julia's parents would be home, though Finn was not sure he could walk that far, anyway.

When two-thirty came and went, his worry turned to real anxiety.

I've got to do something, he said to himself. A clap of thunder broke and rolled, nearer than before.

I'll get the cocaine, then we can start straight for the fort before the storm breaks.

Finn started pulling himself up the stairs, but it was hard work. It hurt. When he limped into his room, he was tired. If his nerves weren't so on edge, he'd be tempted to go back to bed for a while. He couldn't rest now, however; he must be downstairs and ready to go when Julia came.

He pulled open the bureau drawer and suddenly went cold all over. Breathless, pushing the recorder aside, he scuffled frantically through the underclothes in the drawer.

Where is it?

In vain his hands searched every corner of the drawer. Gone.

Realization hit him like a blow, making his cheeks sting as the blood raced back to them: *Julia!*

Julia had taken the packet last night while he slept.

But she promised! Finn felt a tide of rage rise from his gut.

He replayed their conversation the evening before and was torn between fury and an unwanted tenderness.

She did it for me, he thought. *She's planning to take it back for me.* Finn thought his heart might shatter like a Christmas tree ball.

For the first time lightning preceded the thunder. It flashed across the afternoon sky, turning the darkened little attic room briefly white. Seconds later another wave of thunder broke and rolled over the valley. Still no rain. The air was thick with it, but it didn't fall.

Finn stumbled to the door; twice he nearly fell down the stairs in his haste to reach the kitchen door.

He tore it open and looked out. No bicycle.

So she hasn't taken it back to the fort. Not yet. Maybe, pray God, maybe she took it back last night. Or maybe home. Maybe she is home, now, waiting for the storm to pass.

But she would have called me. He tried not to think about that.

He went to the phone and dialed her number from memory.

The phone rang and rang. What he would do if someone else answered it by chance, Finn did not know. *Grunt*, he guessed. He knew how to grunt.

Lightning flashed again. Still a pause before thunder. The storm was not yet overhead. Finn hung up the phone and started for the door, dragging the cast behind him.

The barn: maybe she stopped off in the barn. Maybe one of the twins is sick, or Daisy—maybe Daisy what? Got kicked or something. Or maybe

Hiram lost a shoe and she went to look for it in the pasture . . .

It seemed to take forever to get to the barn. Every muscle in his body protested. Finn gritted his teeth and stumbled on. When he reached the barn door and saw that Julia was not there, he very nearly wept with anxiety and frustration. Where could she be?

Then, as he stood bewildered by indecision, a rattling noise made him look toward the toolshed. When it came again, he crossed the patch of grass to investigate, and Monica ran out the door with a mouse in her jaws. At the same moment Finn's eye fell on the edge of a wheel. Even before he reached it, he knew it was the wheel of Julia's bicycle. He had to struggle to bring back his breath.

This is awful. This is truly, truly awful. She's done it. She's taken it to the fort. She's been up there all this time . . .

He lurched back across the stretch of grass to the barn door.

Keep moving, Finn told himself, *just keep moving, and this won't catch up with you.*

But suddenly he couldn't keep moving. He had nowhere to go. No way to get there.

Helplessness swamped him, leaving him as paralyzed and lost as he'd been in the Absarokas. Now it was Julia who was lost and he was powerless to save her—as powerless as he had been when he let his family die in flames. As powerless as when the coyote had chewed his father's hand . . . Oh God, oh God, here came the terror—he could feel it rising in him like a poisonous gas.

Sheet lightning flickered once, twice, then flared full force, turning the barnyard white. This time the thunder followed immediately, crackling and rumbling over Riverview Farm. He heard the horses moving restlessly in the shed. A few warm, fat drops splashed heavily onto Finn's face, as though to remind him of something, and, like the lightning in the sky, an idea flashed in his mind:

I'll ride *to her!* he thought.

Buoyed by relief to have his mind function again, he dragged himself into the barn. All was clear, now: He would catch Belle. Bridle her. No problem there.

Lift on the saddle? Even reaching for the bridle inside the barn door tore at all his muscles. Never mind, he'd ride bareback.

Finn started down the barn for the gate to the shed, the bridle over one arm, reviewing each step of his plan. He would swing onto Belle's bare back from the top fence rail and ride across the pasture to the far gate. He was sure the well-trained mare would stand so that he could open the gate while mounted. Then he would ride to the fort and— Panic froze his thoughts again.

Don't think. Just keep moving. One thing at a time. One moment at a time. One step at a time.

All the horses stood in the shed; all four heads turned as one to regard Finn. He opened the gate and went in to them and, moving slowly, as he had seen

Julia do, limped up to Belle and laid his free hand on the long silver nose.

Daisy came up behind him and nibbled daintily at Finn's shirt. Hiram and Horace stood watching the proceedings through half-closed eyes. The air was sultry, heavy with still-unshed rain. In the goat pen, Vetch bleated for attention.

Finn raised the bridle over Belle's ears and gave her the bit just as fork lightning streaked across the sky, illuminating the whole horizon and ushering in a loud, slow roll of thunder.

The stone well rose like an island out of a lake of thin smoke. Here and there miniature waves of flame broke the surface of the banked pine needles. Appearing briefly and at random, they disappeared again under the forest floor, only to emerge somewhere else. In this manner they spread in ever-widening ripples through the pinewood, casting smoke before them.

Toq smelled it right away. It terrified him. Over the soft licking noises of the flames human cries reached his ears. Belly low, he hurried through the pinewood toward the fort and stopped dead.

A voice rose from the depths of the well. It was the girl and she was keening.

Toq was torn between his own terror of the spreading fire and the girl's need. All his instincts told him to flee, that the hidden tongues of flame were spreading slow but sure through the whole pinewood. Already he had seen the other denizens of the wood leaving. Birds, voles, a single coyote—the one that often spied on the goats at Riverview Farm—these and others of the woods' sparse population ran from the fearsome, rising smoke.

Again the cry from the well.

A little tongue of fire rose up and lapped at Toq's leg. Retreating, it sank below the needles and hugged the ground, moving on invisibly. Smoke thickened the dank air. Overhead, thunder rolled again and again, louder and louder, each crash heralded now by jagged bursts of light. Toq heard heavy drops begin to fall on the unseen upper limbs of the pines.

He stood motionless for a moment more. Then, when he heard the girl's futile attempt to throw herself up the wall, he made his decision. He turned and fled, knowing only that he must find the boy. So intent was he on his mission that he never smelled the body lying just off the path nor saw the flames playing over the thinning reddish hair.

The raindrops were smaller now and fell faster. They stung the scar on Finn's face and soaked his heavy hair. Belle stood quietly while he struggled up the rails of the fence. It seemed to take forever before he straddled the top one and another eternity to mount the mare. Three times he tried to swing his bad leg over her back. Finally, grunting with pain, he was astride. He took up the reins and Belle immediately moved off toward the far gate.

Halfway there, both smelled the smoke. The mare stopped and snorted. At first Finn's mind could not process the smell. *I am imagining smoke*, he told himself, and he shook the rain out of his hair and urged Belle on. The mare stepped forward reluctantly, then stopped again and stared straight ahead. Finn looked up, and through the falling rain he saw the wolf-dog standing in the opening of the path.

At the bottom of the well Julia coughed and gasped. When first she had smelled the woodsmoke, she thought she must have dreamed it, because there was no trace of it in the narrow circle that was her only sky. Then, bit by bit, little tendrils had crept through the stone sides of the well, about halfway between where she sat and the top.

I must not breathe deep, she said to her pounding heart. *Lie low. Lie low. Put your face on the bottom and breathe in and out against the stones.*

She did as she told herself, but as she lay sprawled face-down against the rocky floor, tears slid out from under her closed lids.

Please, she prayed. *Please help me.*

She would not call again until all the air was gone.

Toq barked, once, a deep guttural noise that Finn had never heard any animal make before. As he stared transfixed at the wild animal, a wisp of smoke billowed out of the wood next to the gate and tainted the air with its stench. Finn's flesh prickled.

Smoke, that is smoke, he told himself. *I am not imagining it at all.*

Toq barked again, then turned away from Belle and Finn and headed up the path.

When they did not follow, he returned and stared at them again, whining, seeming with this strange new sound to call to them. Finn felt Belle trembling under him, but she took one step after another toward the gate. On the other side the entrance to the pinewood lay, several yards to the right.

Finn leaned over, holding Belle's mane with his good hand, and unhitched the chain that held the gate shut. As he did so, he was struck again by the pinkness of his burned fingers. For so long they had worn the black glove that Finn almost felt they belonged on another hand. The mare, her silver coat turned to pewter by the downpour of rain, stepped through the gate. Another fork of lightning split the sky. The following crash of thunder, directly overhead, made them both jump. Wind rose to drive the rain in horizontal sheets. Finn put up his arm to shield his face and squeezed Belle's sides with his knees.

Again the wolf-dog appeared at the mouth of the path. The smoke had thickened considerably. It billowed around Toq, making him pant with the fear of it. Once again he gave his deep imperious bark.

"Come!" he seemed to say.

Whining and growling, he backed toward the path, leading, urging, cajoling them to follow him. Again

Finn squeezed Belle's sides and she broke obediently into a trot. When they got to the entrance to the wood, they saw the fire bursting through the bed of needles on either side. The miniature flames looked innocent and lighthearted, like fairies dancing under the trees, but Finn felt his bowels turn to water at the sight.

Fire!

His mind catapulted to the Wyoming mountainside. It was there again, before his very eyes, the fearful, burning plane. Fire erupted everywhere, crackling and muffling the sound of voices crying for help.

"Finn!" called his father, and Finn struggled to drag his broken body toward the fire.

"Almost there, I'm coming, I'm coming," he wanted to shout, but could not, could not shout, only crawl, crawl, crawl toward the flames, hearing beyond the crackling noise they made the high, faint sound of another voice.

Who called? Whose voice was that? Where was his own? "I'm coming, I am here," he wanted to tell them, but he couldn't, he didn't; they never knew he was there. If only I could tell them I was there, if only I could believe that they knew I was there. Oh, God, I was there, but you never knew . . .

He was seized by a desire to run, run, run away from the fire and the fear. He gathered up the reins to turn back, and as he did so the whole world turned white and a new and endless-seeming surge of thunder rolled across the sky.

Belle flinched. For a moment she hesitated, mesmerized by the boy's fear and her own, until, as the thunder finally trailed off toward the east, a pitiful thin wail rose out of the heart of the smoking wood.

"Finn! Finn! *Finn!*"

In that instant something happened. Time stopped. The world around Finn faded away; the smoke, the fire, the storm—they all blurred. Without moving he found himself in that place that has no bounds, but only power and acquiescence.

I have found my way back, he knew. *I am here, now, I am here, in the very heart of my fort, and the walls are tumbling down, down, down. The walls are tumbling down and I am here, I am home and I am not alone: There is a voice here with me at the heart of my heart—it is my voice.*

Julia! he cried out in his mind. His throat moved convulsively. It ached with the effort he made, but no sound came.

Again: *Julia!* A noise this time, like the pigs at feed, but a noise nonetheless.

Oh, God. His voice . . . Fear clutched him again.

I can't, I can't. What was I thinking of?

Lightning blazed across the sky, pulsing whiter and whiter, illuminating the farm, the river, the valley, the world, illuminating *his* world, his strange familiar place. And again, through the thunder, came the high wail: "Finn!"

Deep, deep he drew his breath, past the awful cork, filling his lungs and filling his entire self until it throbbed with a substance like light, and with a mighty shout, he roared, louder than the thunder he roared, *"JULIA!"*

The sound of his own voice burst his heart wide open.

"Julia!" he called again. *"Julia, we're coming!"* And he laid his head on Belle's neck and urged her into the burning wood.

Jack could hardly see the road through the rain. It fell in torrents, making a mockery of his windshield wipers.

Jeezus, what a day, he groaned to himself for the twentieth time.

Rafe had skipped town. No one in Ludlow knew where he was. The last three people Jack talked to said they'd seen Rafe heading south in a Ford Escort, with a stranger at the wheel. No one knew who the stranger was, no one knew where they were headed.

He's gone, that double-dealing sucker. Jack was almost crying with rage and frustration. *Now what the hell am I supposed to do?*

A massive bolt of lightning blinded him and the roar that followed took his breath away. He wanted to pull off the road until the rain stopped, but he couldn't stop thinking about that girl Julia in the well . . . And Pinky, well, he guessed Pinky was home free now that Rafe was gone.

What a business. Never again, Jack swore to himself. *Never again.*

Up the narrow smoking path Belle struggled. Eyes fixed on the wolf-dog, she followed him, half trotting, half galloping. Branches scratched her flanks and twice tendrils of flame lapped across the path, ducking out of sight again before they singed Belle's legs. Belle heard them crackle as they went—here, there, nearly invisible, yet everywhere, filling the air with smoke and striking primitive terror into her heart. But she never wavered.

Through all the noise of storm and fire came Julia's voice, "Here. Here at the fort. Oh, Finn, come! Hurry!" She coughed and gasped.

Belle scrambled blindly on toward the voice. When they got to the well, Finn slipped off her back and only then did she hang her head low, heaving for breath. One after the other she picked her hooves up and down, seeking relief from the heated trail.

Finn flung himself to the wall and leaned far over the edge.

"Give me your hand," he shouted.

Moaning, Julia stretched to her full length, but could not reach his groping fingers.

Finn extended his long body farther into the well. "Again, try again. Take my hand. Jump!"

Julia backed off and leaped with all the strength left in her. Their fingers touched, but could not hold, and she fell back with a cry of frustration and lay gasping for breath on the stones. Lightning flared; thunder crashed.

Finn pushed himself away from the well and stared wildly around him. The half-dead trunks of the pines were beginning to smoke. Finn seized the first long branch he could reach. It snapped off in his hand, and again he hung over the edge. His feet no longer touching the ground, he held the branch out to Julia with his good hand. She grabbed it and hung on. Inch by inch, dancer's feet hugging the wall, she crept toward him. When her fingers closed around his wrist, he dropped the branch and grabbed her hand with both of his.

"Good, good, good," he gasped. "Keep coming. You're nearly there."

Finn was sure that either his arm would break or Julia would pull him down into her dungeon, until suddenly he was aware that something tugged his leg. Briefly he turned his head and saw the wolf-dog straining backward. His powerful jaws were locked around the bottom of the cast, three paws buried like anchors in the earth, the right front one held high. With the last of her strength, Julia scaled the top of the well and fell into Finn's arms.

Lightning exploded as though celebrating the triumph in the wood. Smoke and thunder melded to blind and deafen them all. Under the heavier rain, the flames sizzled, but, still unextinguished, moved on. And Toq veered off into the smoke. Running low and fast through the flames, he disappeared from their sight.

"*Come back!*" Finn called. In vain. He was gone.

Julia sprang onto Belle's back, then reached out her arms to help Finn climb on behind her. "Run, Belle, run," cried Julia.

Sides heaving, Belle bolted down the path. Her unshod hooves slithered almost out of control beneath her; twice she slid to her haunches. Her breath was almost gone when they burst out of the wood.

Once free of the smoke, Julia drew Belle to a halt. Head low, heart racing, the old mare gulped for air. Julia slid off and put her hand on Belle's throat. Bang, bang, bang, went her heart; and then, pitter-patter, pitter-patter.

"Oh, Belle," Julia sobbed, and her tears ran into the wet gray ear. "Oh, Belle, Belle, Belle, it's all right now. We're safe. You brought us home again."

Two hours later, as though worn out, the lightning simply stopped. Far across the river thunder rumbled, pleasantly low. Standing at the kitchen window, Finn could see rain still falling over there. Here at Riverview Farm an apologetic evening sun cast watery light upon the house and barn. It filtered through the pall of smoke that wafted across the pasture and cast long evening shadows over the lawn. The pinewood still burned, but rain had doused the worst of the fire, and bit by bit the flames subsided. Firemen stood by with shovels as the town ambulance drove by with Pinky's body inside.

A screen door slammed and Finn turned from the window to see the last of the neighbors leave the house. The Hatches had long since borne Julia home to rest. Now only his grandmother stood behind him in the kitchen, and although she did not seem able to stop the tears that rolled down her face, Finn suddenly thought, *She looks like Gram again.* He put his arms around her.

"Tell me again," she said thickly. "Tell me just once more what happened."

"I will, Gram," Finn told her. His voice was rough around the edges, but it didn't flag or waver. "I'll tell you all over again. Again and again. But first I must go see Belle."

Down in the barn the animals sought to recover their composure. The hens were still aflutter. They could not settle down, but fussed at each other in agitated clucks and squawks. Clara hovered over her kids, nuzzling them against her udder. Monica, licking each paw on her beam, waited for the long, long day to end. And in the shed the three old horses stood nose to nose. Tails swishing back and forth, they seemd to confer, while Daisy, exhausted from the stressful afternoon, lay prone and fast asleep on the cool earthen floor.

After a while Belle left the shed. In her sedate and regal way she walked out of the barnyard. Pausing at the pasture gate to catch her breath, she looked back once at her sleeping filly. Then, ears pricked, her head held high, she continued on her way. Very slowly, step by step, she headed for Ben's green grave. When she reached it, she stopped again and gazed across the river. The storm had ended there now; the rolling hills were clear and green under a pale blue sky.

For several minutes Belle stood without moving, until, slowly but very gracefully, she lowered herself onto the lush patch of ungrazed grass. A deep sigh shuddered through her. Her eyelids grew heavy; the long white lashes drooped.

Thump, thump, went her tired old heart . . .

Thump, just one last time.

Rounding the corner of the barn, Finn stopped in midstride. There, right there on the bright green grass that no horse would eat, lay Belle, and Finn knew instantly that she had gone.

Too late. I've come too late.

Limping to the fence, he leaned against it, exhausted. His eyes brimmed: How small her silver body looked, lying so still on Ben's grave.

"I came to thank you, Belle," he said aloud.

For many minutes Finn stood at the pasture fence, gazing at Belle's motionless body. And in that time peace descended upon him like a cloud. Peace seeped into his own body, welled up in his throat, and filled his heart. He closed his eyes and gave thanks.

Then he turned stiffly and started for the house. Halfway up the lane a movement caught his eye. In the twilit hayfield sat Toq, watching him. Finn stopped. His body ached with exhaustion, but he stood there in the lane, looking at the wolf-dog. The evening shadows of the great maples lay like graceful veils across the lawn between them.

"Come," Finn called softly.

Toq got to his feet, took a step forward, then sank to his haunches again, shivering a little.

"No hurry," said Finn. "It just takes time . . . I'll be waiting for you."